CHOSEN WOLF

THE MARKED WOLF TRILOGY

JEN L. GREY

Copyright © 2021 by Jen L. Grey

All rights reserved.

No part of this book may be reproduced in any form or by any electronic or mechanical means, including information storage and retrieval systems, without written permission from the author, except for the use of brief quotations in a book review.

CHAPTER ONE

Emma

Dealing with dead bodies at five a.m. wasn't my ideal start to a good day. The sky was still dark, and none of us had gotten any sleep since the wolf attack and the earthquake I'd caused.

I could've stayed back to help the witches pack all the houses and load the cars, but this was where I needed to be. After all, this was all my fault. If I hadn't come here, the coven would still be thriving—not rushing to leave before a secret society arrived to kill us all. Ten witches and twenty wolves were dead because of me. I couldn't let any more people die.

The thick metallic scent of blood hung in the air, and flies buzzed around the bodies. I regretted my decision to help bury the dead, but damn, how could I be a good leader if I didn't take on the hard jobs?

The irony was that the wolves expected me to ruin them, and the witches expected me to save them.

Me.

I was supposed to be the witches' hero, their redeemer, but I was clueless, which was far more dangerous.

I'd only survived this long because of my mate, whose pack was part of the secret society, and my four new witch friends: Samuel, Amethyst, Coral, and Finn. Without them, I'd be rotting in the ground.

Holding my breath, I grabbed the dead man's arms and dragged him across the grass toward the woods. My arms screamed because the guy had at least two hundred pounds on me. The Jones pack had sent their strongest and most skilled shifters to kill me. I wondered if my ex-boyfriend and the pack's alpha heir, Jacob Rogers, even knew who his roommate really was. Prescott Jones was part of a secret society seeking the wolf marked by the witches who so happened to be me.

Aidan walked over and touched my arm. "You don't have to do this." His golden eyes locked with mine, and the gentle buzzing of our fated mate bond thrummed through my skin at his touch. "Go back to the house and pack up. We'll head back when we're done." His muscular chest brushed against my arm as he tried pulling the dead shifter from my grasp.

"No, I need to do this. They came here for me." I wanted to scream and yell. This was my burden and no one else's, but that wouldn't accomplish anything. I couldn't do this on my own.

Hell, I hadn't even processed that I was half witch. I'd grown up a wolf shifter my entire life, and even though I was adopted, it had never crossed my mind that I could be something more. The Rogers pack took me in after they'd found me as an infant at the border, lying next to a dead wolf.

"Emma, you don't have to," Aidan said slowly, as though he were choosing his words carefully.

Annoyance flared through me. He'd already said that. I used our mate bond connection to mind link with him. *I'm expected to lead.* He had to understand, and I didn't want to embarrass him in front of everyone. *I can't do that by running away when things get hard.*

"She already told you she does. It's her choice." Finn, my newly found cousin, shoved Aidan hard in the chest. His hate-filled amber eyes landed on my mate.

"You're damn lucky you're her family," Aidan growled as he removed Finn's hands from his chest. "Otherwise, you'd be on your back right now."

"See, that's my problem with all you animals. You think you're so bad. If you try that alpha-will shit on her, you'll be treated like that shifter I killed in the basement last night. It was nice to see his cockiness leave as he took his last breath."

He obviously had issues with wolves since they'd killed his parents. My only saving grace with him was that I was his cousin and half witch, even though that was recent news. However, he was still cold toward Aidan and my best friend, Beth. He couldn't look past them being wolves ... at least not yet.

Beth joined us, catching the end of the conversation. "That's messed up," Beth mumbled beside me. "He's almost glowing at the memory."

"I am not." Finn shook his head, causing his auburn hair to fall against his forehead. "Witches aren't meant to cause harm unless absolutely necessary. I didn't enjoy it, but it was justice."

Samuel reached our group, dragging one of the dead shifters. "We all need to calm down." He dropped the guy he'd been carrying back on the ground, and the body landed with a loud thud. Crimson blood spotted his chestnut hair that was pulled back into a man bun, making his sage eyes brighter ... and spooky. "We're all on edge after the fight." He blew out a breath and winced as if to rid himself of the memories. "And we're running on no sleep. We can't turn on one another."

"Just to be clear, I would never try to control her." Anger laced Aidan's words, but he stopped and sucked in some air.

"Besides, it wouldn't work if he tried." I kept my voice light to tamp down some of the tension. My attention focused on Finn. "Remember, he's your family now, too." I pointed to the almost healed bite mark on my neck.

"Don't remind me," Finn huffed.

"He also knows I'd help kick his ass if he tried controlling my girl." Beth's blue hair bobbed with each step she took. She moved to throw her arm over my shoulders, but I stepped out of the way. Blood stained her hands from the man she'd hauled into the woods.

Hurt appeared on her face.

Great, now I was making people feel bad. I didn't want more blood on me than necessary. "Sorry, but I don't want to completely ruin my clothes." Another run to the local Walmart was imminent.

Her gaze flicked to the man at my feet, and she tilted her head. "Yeah, I don't blame you there."

Aidan grabbed the arm of the guy I'd been trying to move.

"Hey, I said I've got it." After all that, he still decided to pull this shit. Even though I'd been struggling with the shifter, I didn't like how Aidan was handling the situation.

"There's one over there." He pointed to a guy who was

slightly smaller and a little less bloody since only his throat had been ripped out.

I wanted to stand my ground but knew I'd look stupid if I did. I'd probably have trouble carrying this one too. I made my way to the other body and hollered at Beth, "Want to help?"

"Not really, but I will." She took hold of his legs while I grabbed his arms.

We slowly lifted him and made our way to the woods.

Tears threatened, but I refused to let them spill. Those wolves had come here to kill. If we hadn't fought back, they would've killed more of us. The attack had happened right before I'd unleashed my witch power. If that was a sign of what was to come, I wasn't sure fate had made the right choice in picking me.

The witches were trying to be strong, but I could see the toll the conflict was taking, especially on the ones who'd chosen to help bury the attackers. I felt a kinship with them. Though I was part animal and enjoyed being the hunter, I didn't enjoy the kill.

I held my breath again to keep the scent of werewolf blood out of my nose as much as possible. The scent would be scarred into my mind for a very long time.

"Hey, it'll be okay," Beth whispered so only I could hear. "They don't blame you."

"They should." I would find a way to make things right. If I'd stayed away, the wolves never would've attacked them.

"No, they shouldn't." Beth rolled her eyes. "And it's not like wolves never attack witches. Even if our packs got along with them, there are several other packs that hate them. Your mate's being one of them."

That was why Aidan had walked away from me over four years ago. Right after our first kiss, he'd seen my mark—

a birthmark of a star, or a pentagram as the witches called it—and disappeared from my life until we ran into each other at the university. Only a couple of days had passed since he'd turned his back on his pack to be with me.

As if my thoughts had called him to me, Aidan stepped from the woods right as we reached the tree line. He moved toward me as if to take my place.

I mind linked with him. *I've got this. Please don't keep pushing.*

He frowned but nodded. *I just hate seeing you deal with this. I'm supposed to protect you.*

No, you're supposed to stand beside me and treat me as an equal. I understood his instinct. Hell, I even had the same one toward him, but being overprotective of each other wasn't possible in this new world of mine. *To get through the coming months, I need you to get on board.*

He huffed. *You're right, but I'm not happy about it.*

Never said you had to be. I winked and dropped the conversation. Now wasn't the time to celebrate our bond.

I'll go help Samuel and Finn with the last few. He headed off toward the male witches.

I wasn't sure that was the smartest idea, but they would have to learn to work together. Beth and I took a foot trail and found five male witches digging the last three graves. Ugh. There were twenty in total—one for each shifter.

"Take him over to Mom." Amethyst's face was lined with dirt, which made her dark violet eyes appear haunted. Her body sagged as she ran her hand through her dirty blonde hair and picked up her shovel again. Even though she was petite, she plunged the shovel into the loose dirt and began burying the dead shifter.

Beth groaned. "I'm still surprised we're taking the time to do this before we get out of here."

"Everyone deserves to be placed back in the ground. It's more out of respect for Mother Nature, and we pray that they find peace despite experiencing such a violent demise." Beatrice, the coven's priestess, placed a hand on her heart as her blonde and gray hair spilled down her face. "I've never seen anything like it in all my years."

"Hopefully we won't have to see it again." I meant those words, but a prickly stab of fear latched onto my skin. I was terrified that I might see so much worse in the very near future."

"Bring him right over here, girls." Beatrice waved us over. Even though she wasn't shoveling, dirt still smeared her face. "We need to hurry. The pack will begin searching for their members and catch their trail soon, and we need to be out of here." Dark circles lightened her purple eyes.

Between tracking their cell phones and all of the other modern technology, it wouldn't take them long to find their cars and track their scent right to us.

"Anything else we can do to help? The guys are getting the last three—" I winced before I could say the rest. "—bodies, and we should be ready to head back and pack."

"The sun is about to rise, and the pack will be on the hunt soon. Luckily, we've been preparing for this moment. Most of the coven should already be on their way home," Beatrice said as she stood tall, stretching her back. "Sage, Rowan, and Coral should have most of our things packed if not everything."

"Home?" That struck me as odd. Even though they didn't have many items, I'd figured this was their home.

"Yes, it'll be nice to be back where we belong." A small smile teased the corners of her mouth.

"Why don't you all head back up now?" The older man who was digging the grave pointed at us. "I'll finish this up while Agatha and Tulip finish packing things. We'll be done in the next thirty minutes." Sincerity filled his cobalt blue eyes.

"All right. You three be safe on the drive down. Call me if you need anything." She turned and waved at us to follow. "Let's go."

The four of us returned to the houses in amicable silence. Truth be told, we might've kept quiet from exhaustion.

When we broke through the tree line, we found Finn with a shifter over his shoulders. Blood dripped down the guy's face and onto the grass. The blood looked sticky and cold instead of warm and runny.

Vomit threatened to come up my throat, but somehow, I kept it down.

"Hurry up." Beatrice's hands shook as she took in the area. Blood coated everything, even the trees. "We need to get out of here."

"Yes, ma'am." Finn nodded and picked up his pace to the graves.

I hurried past him, and thankfully, Samuel and Aidan were being more careful, dragging the guys by their feet.

I focused on Aidan. "We're going to help finish packing."

"Okay, cool," Samuel groaned. "We'll be ready soon."

"We all need a shower." Blood clung to me, and I needed to get the smell out of my nose.

"That is a very true statement." Beth pointed at me. "I'll go to Coral's and Rowan's to get clean and grab my things. Shouldn't take longer than ten minutes."

"Time is of the essence." Amethyst stilled as if she sensed something no one else did. "They'll be here soon. I feel it in my bones."

Dread filled my stomach. We had to make it out before more wolves arrived. Next time, I wasn't sure we could fight them off.

Aidan

"Surprised you stayed to help us witches since Emma left," Finn said with hatred.

I was getting so damn tired of his comments. I got that my pack had killed his parents, but that wasn't me. I'd been a newborn. It was so hard keeping my mouth shut, but I was doing it for Emma. He was her family, probably the only biological family she would ever have, and I was trying to make it as easy as possible for them to have a relationship. I'd turned to focus on another body when Finn grabbed my arm.

"Dude, come on." Samuel sighed. "Yes, he was an ass to us at first, but he grew up hating us like you've grown up hating them. He stayed behind to help, for Goddess's sake."

Instead of listening to his friend, his hand tightened.

"You better back off." I wouldn't fight him, but I had to stand my ground somewhat. My wolf was surging forward, wanting me to put him in his place.

"Or what?" Finn sneered. "You'll kill me like you did my parents."

"No, asshole." I worked to keep my wits. This guy was asking for a beating, but I had to remember Emma. "But I won't keep letting you push me around." I grabbed his hand and squeezed, slackening his grip. Then, I shoved him away. "The only reason I haven't beaten the shit out of you is because of one girl who is important to both of us. But if you keep pushing, I'll bite."

Finn's jaw clenched, but Samuel came over to stand between us.

Samuel took a step toward him. "What the fuck are you doing?"

"See ... he threatened me." Finn's body shook with rage. "I told you we couldn't trust them."

"He was protecting himself," Samuel said as he shoved his friend in the chest, making Finn fall back a few steps. "You're being an aggressive asshole."

I turned my back, showing him I didn't fear him in the least. Yes, it went against everything in my nature, but if I treated him like a threat, he would act worse. "Unlike you, I'm well aware that, to protect the coven, we need to finish the job and get out of here." I picked up the dead guy's legs and glanced over my shoulder at Finn. "Unless you're the one who doesn't care about keeping them safe."

Finn's eyes narrowed with hatred, but he couldn't say anything to that.

"He's right. The longer we're here, the riskier it is." Samuel motioned to the guy next to Finn. "Now, let's get to work."

Samuel siding with me didn't make the situation better, but Finn had to realize I wasn't his punching bag. Eventually, I'd strike back.

CHAPTER TWO

Emma

After my shower, I still felt numb and floaty. The past twenty-four hours had changed everything for me. I didn't even feel like the same person.

As I toweled off, I tried thinking about anything other than last night, but it was impossible. The mirror was fogged from my shower, so I reached over the sink to wipe the condensation away. The reflection staring back at me was almost unrecognizable. My olive skin seemed a tad lighter, which darkened my gray eyes. Even the cleft of my chin seemed more pronounced.

I ran a brush through my long blonde hair and turned my head to the right, moving my hair aside. I looked at the black birthmark of a star. It looked more like a tattoo than a birthmark now that I was really taking the time to examine it, but it had been there since I was a baby girl.

The door to the bedroom opened, and Aidan stepped inside. He turned his head toward the bathroom where I was standing. Blood and dirt marked his face, but he still looked handsome.

"I could get used to walking into a room and finding you naked." He grinned, causing my insides to burn. "If we weren't in a hurry, I'd coax you back into the shower."

"That is tempting, so I'll take a rain check," I said as I made my way into the room and picked up a pale blue bra from the bed. Sex would be an amazing distraction. Last night flashed through my mind. It had been the first time for both of us, and it had been more amazing than I had ever thought possible. No matter how much I wished we could enjoy another round, it wasn't possible. The wolves could arrive at any moment.

"I'll be quick." He headed into the bathroom, turned the water on, and stripped.

It was physically impossible for me not to watch the show. His body was muscular and something to marvel at. "Sounds good. I'll begin packing." We didn't have much, so it would only take me a few minutes.

When he stepped into the shower, I focused on getting dressed.

By the time he got out of the shower, I was ready and had everything packed except for the clothes and towels we were leaving behind.

He quickly changed into a pair of jeans and a black shirt. He grabbed my waist and pulled me into his chest. "Are you okay?" His eyes lightened to a near yellow.

"No." I wouldn't lie to him. Hell, even if I'd wanted to, he'd know. That was one of the pains about being a shifter. The sulfur smell was our tell. "But with you by my side, I'll make it." I had to.

"There is no place in the world I'd rather be."

The fact it wasn't a lie put some of my paranoia at

ease. I only hoped that one day in the future, he still wouldn't regret choosing me over his family. I hadn't made him choose—it had been his brother—but still. Family was important. No one knew that better than an orphan.

"Hey," he said as he touched my face, bringing me back to the present. "What's wrong?"

"I hope you still feel the same way in ten years." I hated being vulnerable, but losing him was my worst fear.

"I swear to you I will." He leaned down and touched his lips to mine. After a second, he pulled back, his minty breath hitting my face. "I'm all in, in case you can't tell by now."

A slow grin spread across my face. "Good, because I'd hate to hunt you down."

"Keep threatening and I may just cause more trouble." He kissed me once more.

A loud howl broke whatever small spell we'd been under.

They were almost here.

Aidan grabbed the tote with our stuff and ran to the door. "We've got to go."

Without missing a beat, I followed behind him, and we raced down the stairs to where Amethyst and Beatrice waited.

Amethyst was holding the door open as Beatrice rolled out a suitcase from her room.

"We need to figure out which cars are left over," Beatrice said in a panic.

"We'll take my car." Aidan motioned her on. "I don't want my dad to find my car here anyway. I'm sure the two packs are working together now." He reached into his pocket and took out his cell phone. He threw it hard on the ground, smashing it. "And now Dad can't track me if he gets desperate enough to try."

"Okay then," Beatrice agreed. "We need to check on the others."

"We're good." Amethyst smiled as we ran out the door. "Beth, Coral, and Rowan are taking the Honda. Finn, Samuel, and Sage are taking their truck."

As she spoke, we saw the rest of our group running from the houses to the cars like Amethyst had described. We all rushed to Aidan's car, and he opened the trunk.

Another howl sounded no more than a mile away. They were taunting us, expecting us to cower in fear.

"What about the older man who was shoveling?" It didn't feel right to leave anyone behind.

"They left a few minutes ago." Beatrice hurried to the rear passenger door. "We're the last ones."

"You can sit up front." It felt disrespectful for me to take the front seat.

"We don't have time for this." Aidan pointed to the tree line as a dark wolf appeared. "Get in now."

Not bothering to worry any longer, the four of us got into the Jeep. As soon as the last door closed, Aidan squealed out of the driveway and headed straight toward the wolf.

The other two vehicles pulled out and filed in behind us.

The wolf ran toward the road, and as soon as he reached it, two others came into view.

"Shit," Aidan grumbled as he gunned the car.

"What's wrong?" I feared that the wolf wouldn't move. Would he sacrifice himself for the cause?

"That's Bradley." His strained voice rang clear. "I smashed the damn phone too late. Bradley called Dad, and they fucking tracked me. That's how they found us so damn fast."

His brother intended to force him to stop the car and turn me, his fated mate, over. What kind of asshole would force his own flesh and blood to either run over family or hand over his mate?

"Who's Bradley?" Beatrice's voice shook.

"My brother." He sighed but didn't let up on the gas.

"Just pull over. I'll get out willingly." I didn't want Aidan to live with killing his own brother.

Aidan didn't respond, but his knuckles turned white from his grip on the steering wheel.

"Seriously." If he thought I was testing him, I wasn't.

"Emma, you know he won't turn you over to them," Amethyst said softly. She touched my shoulder. "He'll always pick you."

Bradley stared Aidan down from the middle of the road.

My heart hammered in my ears.

We were only about two car lengths away. Something like fear appeared in Bradley's animal eyes.

I'd braced for the inevitable impact when, at the very last second, Bradley stepped out of the car's path. The air from the vehicle passing ruffled his fur.

Although we'd missed him, adrenaline still pumped through me. I turned around in time to see the other two vehicles rush by him.

A howl filled the air as we flew down the gravel roadway, rocks flying in every direction.

"Oh, thank Goddess." Beatrice sighed with relief. "I'm not sure I can handle more blood today."

"Me neither." Amethyst leaned her head back against the seat.

Even though they were relieved, I wasn't sure we were out of the woods yet ... figuratively and literally.

I sat on the edge of the seat and scanned the trees. Every now and then, it appeared like a wolf was running in our direction, but we were going too fast for it to catch up.

Between that and making sure the cars behind us weren't attacked, my head began to hurt.

Most of the shifters would be heading toward the subdivision. They weren't aware that all the witches were gone.

A huge wolf stood on a gradual hilltop, his eyes on our car as if he had to see us scurry away.

Aidan

MY FATHER APPEARED, which didn't surprise me. After seeing Bradley, I'd had a feeling he'd be here.

My dad used our pack link to connect with me. *You would've run over your brother for that abomination from the Rogers pack that is sitting beside you?*

I told him I wouldn't stop. I wouldn't let my family manipulate me any longer. *So it was on him.*

You need to stop and hand her over to us. Dad sounded angry. *Before you can't turn back.*

She's my fated mate and nothing like the evil you painted all my life. The longer I was connected with him, the easier it would be for him to follow us.

You've let her mess with your mind. Now, Dad's voice was loud and commanding. I felt the alpha will lace his words. *Stop now. It's time to end her.*

This was the choice I'd never wanted to have to make, but in hindsight, this was my destiny as much as it was hers.

I refused to bow to his will and glanced at him one last time as my father. *You're not my alpha any longer.*

Then, my pack bond disappeared and left behind a cold void that rocked me to the core. But I'd be fine as long as Emma survived.

Emma

AIDAN'S EYES met that of the wolf on the hill, and they stared at each other until the wolf was out of our view.

"We're okay now." Aidan's hands relaxed on the steering wheel.

"Are you sure?" I wished I felt as confident as he did. "That huge-ass wolf was watching us."

"That's how I know we're in the clear." Aidan cleared his throat and looked in the rearview mirror. "That was my father. He always brings up the rear."

I didn't know what I'd been expecting, but it wasn't that. "Oh." Sometimes, I wished words came easier for me.

The car remained silent, and Aidan soon slowed down so we weren't driving so recklessly. When we pulled out onto the main road, I finally began to calm down.

"We should listen to the news." Beatrice fidgeted in the backseat, trying to get comfortable.

"Yeah, I wonder what they're saying about the earthquake last night." Amethyst motioned to the radio. "Do you mind?"

"Nope, not a problem." I scanned the radio stations, looking for the news. Finally, I landed on a news station.

A female voice came on the radio. "I'm sure everyone is aware of what happened last night, but if you're living under a rock, let me tell you. An earthquake was felt across the entire United States around one a.m. eastern standard time. But this was no ordinary earthquake."

"Of course it wasn't." Aidan reached over the center console to take my hand.

The lady continued. "This nine-point-two earthquake was the first one this strong ever recorded, but oddly, there were no foundational issues anywhere. There are no broken windows or fallen buildings. Hell, not even places where the earth split. As a precaution, there are tsunami alerts in place until later this evening."

"There won't be any tsunamis," Beatrice reassured. "This was the witch's power being unleashed from the dead. It was supernatural."

The woman paused. "What has scientists most confused is that there wasn't one area of origin, but rather, it came from the entire United States."

Amethyst leaned back. "I can't wait to see what Emma becomes."

"Where should I be heading?" Aidan asked. "I'm assuming the others headed somewhere."

"Yes, we have a place four hours from here," Amethyst breathed the words. "I can't wait to get back to my real room."

"Wait, that wasn't your home?" Aidan glanced in the rearview mirror.

He hadn't been there earlier when I'd asked, but it made sense that that wasn't where they planned to stay since they lived very minimally.

"Oh, no." Beatrice placed her hands in her lap. "We always worried they'd find us after your mom and dad. We relocated all of our belongings in Columbus, Georgia and moved several hours away, waiting for a sign to return home." She glanced at me. "We now have our sign."

"I hope you're not wrong about that." I might be their beacon of hope, but I didn't have a clue what to do or how to lead. For the past four years, I'd been complaisant. That couldn't be a good thing for a true leader.

"She's scared she's not strong enough," Amethyst said.

"I'm not." They had to see what I was before they got hurt or worse. "For most of my life, I've gone along with things, not wanting to make waves. I'm thinking that's not an attribute you're looking for."

"Dear girl." Beatrice narrowed her eyes. "You were a child and needed time to figure out who you are. You're still figuring it out, but you don't see what we do."

"And what's that?" For some reason, I needed to know.

"They see you the same way I do." Aidan squeezed my hand and smiled adoringly. "You're stronger than you realize. You were going to leave my ass if I didn't get my shit together."

"You walked away from me, so it wouldn't have been that hard." That sounded colder than I'd intended.

He winced. "I was fourteen and didn't understand what was happening. All I knew was that you had the mark my parents raised me to hate. I didn't know what to do, so I disappeared."

"I'm sorry." I had to stop throwing that in his face. "I only meant ..."

"Fate had to make it happen." Beatrice's purple eyes turned a shade darker. "It's part of what made you who you are today. You had to go through the gut-wrenching pain of losing your mate so you could recognize real pain and empathize with others. A good leader must feel the pain of her people."

"Maybe, but that was kind of cruel. It felt like I wasn't a whole person." I never could put that into words until now—until the mate bond.

"Because he's literally the other half of your soul," Amethyst said softly. "It's actually very beautiful and romantic. I grew up wishing I had a soul mate out there."

"What do you mean?"

"It's two people who fit so perfectly together that their souls merge. You said you kissed that night he disappeared. That's when your souls connected," Amethyst said dreamily. "Yes, it might have hurt, but look at the love you two share. It's breathtaking."

"Even when I was being an ass at the football game?" Aidan frowned. "It didn't feel so breathtaking then."

"No, I admit you were an ass." She giggled, the sound so light and happy. "But it was because you were both fighting something that couldn't be fought. You are redeeming yourself, so don't worry."

"How do I become the person I need to be?" That's the one question I needed answered.

"That, dear girl, will take time," Beatrice reassured. "But you're already making strides. The first part will be finding the other girls. You weren't meant to do this alone."

That we could agree on, but something tugged on my heart. How was I supposed to save them all when I didn't even know what to expect?

CHAPTER THREE

We remained silent in the car for at least thirty minutes. We were driving in circles to make sure no one followed us. The last thing we needed was to bring the wolves to the new location, especially since the witches considered that one home.

It was close to seven in the morning, and we hadn't even begun the real drive to Columbus. The sun was rising, and I leaned against the back of the seat, struggling to keep my head up, let alone stay awake.

The combination of Aidan's comforting hand in mine, the lulling sound of the engine, and the adrenaline leaving my body left me feeling too secure. I needed to stay alert and protect everyone.

Right as my body was about to submit to slumber, a loud, shrill sound echoed in the car. It might as well have been a gunshot with how fast I lurched upright and scanned the area for a threat. That's when the noise sounded again.

Aidan's shoulders shook with laughter. "Babe, it's your cell phone."

Great, now I was jumping at harmless things. What a

strong leader I was becoming. I took the phone from my pocket and saw Mom's name. She never called this early, so I was assuming this had something to do with Jacob. I almost ignored the call, but what if she was worried? I straightened my back and swiped ANSWER. "Hello?"

"Emma!" Mom's voice was so loud it hurt my ear.

Their static and background noise alerted me that I was on speakerphone, which meant Dad was also there. Looked like they were springing an intervention on me.

"Hey." I had to be careful. I didn't want to give them information they didn't already know. Protect them and keeping them in the dark as much as possible was a priority. They'd already done so much by taking me in and raising me as their own.

"Where are you?" Dad asked in the quiet voice he reserved for the times he was furious.

"I'm with my friends." That wasn't a lie. Granted, it wouldn't really matter if it was. They couldn't smell it through the phone.

"Maybe someone from the Murphy pack?" Mom accused.

"He turned his back on them for me." They had to see I wasn't being reckless.

"Oh, really?" A scrape filled the line like a chair sliding across the wood floor. "Then I have some ocean-front property to sell you in Kansas."

That's where I'd figured he'd take this conversation. That was his favorite saying when he thought I'd done something stupid. "No, he did."

"Come on, baby girl." Mom cleared her throat. "Guys lie, especially at that age."

Aidan's hand tightened on mine. I hated that he could hear the conversation.

"Mom, he did it right in front of me to both his dad and brother." I couldn't let him talk about Aidan that way. He wasn't a normal guy. He was my fated mate and deserved their respect.

"What about when the alpha comes calling and uses his will on him?" Dad asked.

Okay, so Jacob hadn't told them everything. "His father is the alpha."

Mom gasped. "Are you saying he's a rogue wolf now?"

I hadn't even considered that. Wolves were meant to live in packs. Being rogue drove even the strongest wolves insane. I locked eyes with him. "Are you?"

Technically, no, I'm not. He averted his gaze and stared at the road ahead.

"Of course he'd be right there with you," Dad grumbled. "I take it you stayed together last night?"

I heard my dad speak, but his words weren't the ones I cared about. *Did you reject your dad?*

He sighed and nodded. *I did; otherwise, he could find you.*

The magnitude of everything he'd given up hit me full force. *Aidan ...*

No, that's why I didn't say anything. He squeezed my hand and glanced back at me. *You are the most important thing in my life. My dad and brother would kill you in a heartbeat. I had no choice. I'll always choose you.*

"Emma!" Dad yelled.

"Sorry. What?" Right now, I was more concerned about Aidan than arguing with them.

"Is he a rogue wolf?" he asked more desperately. "If he is, you could be at risk."

You're not. Aidan nibbled on his bottom lip. *Since we're bonded, I'm not alone. My wolf has yours.*

Warmth spread within me. He was right; we were our own pack, even if it was small. "No, he's not."

"So he has another pack to submit to?" Mom's concern bled through her words. "Look, Jacob cares about you. He's willing to take you back ..."

I had to stop her right there. "Mom ..." You know what? They deserved to know. "Aidan is my fated mate."

"This is a joke, right?" Dad said in disbelief.

"No, it's not." They would have to accept it sooner or later.

"Jacob said you'd claim that. Normally, I'd ignore his concern since he's hurting, but this isn't like you." Mom sighed. "Honey, Jacob told us you disappeared a few days ago. Are you in trouble?"

I wanted to laugh hysterically. That was a mild way of describing my situation. "Look, something happened, and it's not safe back at campus."

"What do you mean?" Mom asked with concern.

"You know that birthmark ..." How in the hell did you put something like this into words?

"Of course we do." Dad's voice grew louder as if he'd gotten closer to the phone.

"It means something." I wasn't sure how much I could tell them without putting them in danger.

My dad knows which pack you're from. Aidan grimaced. *He told me before I broke contact. That's why we were staring at each other like that. He was daring me. He won't cross the territory line, but your parents need to be careful.*

Why didn't you tell me earlier? That was information I'd needed pronto.

Because it's early, and your parents are on central time. He frowned. *You were tired, and I was going to tell you after you'd gotten a couple of hours of sleep. I didn't plan on keeping it from you. I just thought it would be pointless to upset you when you needed rest and couldn't call them yet. They're safe at home.*

He was right, but dammit, it pissed me off. *Next time, I want you to tell me. I don't like us keeping secrets from each other. We need to be in this all the way together.* I wouldn't bring it up again, but he'd kept a secret from me for four years. It wasn't his fault, and now I understood why he'd disappeared, but it had left its mark on me.

Okay. He nodded. *I promise.*

"Emma." Mom huffed. "Are you going to tell us or not?"

"Yeah, sorry." I wasn't sure how they would react to the news. Even though our pack didn't mind witches, they still frowned upon a shifter dating someone outside of their race. "It's just ..." I had to rip it off like a Band-Aid. "I'm half witch."

"What?" Silence fell, and I wasn't sure why. I'd expected a bigger reaction. "That's what the birthmark means."

Dad chuckled as if I'd lost my mind. "How do you know that?"

"That's why the Murphy pack hates us. We protected a witch who got pregnant by the Murphy alpha. She cursed the pack before she died. Apparently, I'm destined to lead both wolves and witches. They want to kill me."

"I knew it was weird that the coven had left. We should've sought answers." Mom sounded borderline hysterical.

"Honey, come on. This is a Murphy member, for God's sake." Dad paused. "He could be telling you that to get you to run away with him. You're smarter than this."

The only sign that Aidan could hear them was the slight frown on his face.

"I'd smell the lie. You know that. And it's not just him." They were getting on my nerves. They weren't really listening to me. They'd called ready to argue. This was how they got when they were concerned about my well-being. "We're with a coven, and they recognized the symbol too."

This silence was different, as if realization had finally dawned on them. "Are you sure they aren't working together?"

"The Murphy pack hates witches." I forced myself to calm down. Getting upset with them would remove any progress I'd just made. "There is no way in hell a Murphy shifter would willingly work with a coven and leave his pack if it wasn't for a good reason."

"And you think that reason is you?" Dad's voice was emotionless like he was talking to someone he didn't care about.

"Stop being a jackass," Mom chastised. "What if it's true? She was left right at the border with a dead wolf next to her."

"It doesn't matter. She's our daughter." Dad's tone was absolute.

"No one is arguing that, Josh." Mom sighed with frustration. "Honey, where are you?"

"I can't tell you." I hated that we were in this situation. It wasn't fair or right, but I was quickly learning that it didn't matter. "You know why."

Tell them you'll be getting a new cell phone. Aidan tightened his hold on my hand. *They would track you that way. We need to get you a new one that's not linked to their account.*

I hadn't even thought about that. If the Murphy pack figured out who my parents were, they could hack our information, and there was no telling what they could get. "I'm tossing this phone. I'll call you when I can."

"Are you sure you're safe?" Mom's voice quavered with fear.

No, I wasn't, but I couldn't let them worry about me. It wouldn't do them any good. The Murphy pack would be watching my pack in case I came home or tried to sneak them out. "Yes, I'm fine." At least, they couldn't smell my lie. "Just don't leave our territory until all of this calms down. I can't have anything happen to you two."

"Honey, I think we should come to you." Dad still sounded skeptical.

"I get that you're concerned, but you could lead them straight to us." I needed to protect them in every way that I could. They'd already done so much for me by giving me a loving home when they didn't have to.

A series of loud knocks came from their end of the line.

"What the ..." Dad's voice grew quieter. I could tell he had raced to the door because I heard it open. "Sam, what's wrong?"

"It's Jacob." Sam's voice broke. He sounded upset. Something must have happened to Jacob. "We need to call Emma."

My stomach churned. "What's going on?"

"Emma!" Sam sounded hopeful. "I need you to go get Jacob and bring him to me."

"I ..." Oh, no. "... can't."

"What do you mean?"

"I'm not close by." He must have gotten hurt because of me. "What happened?"

"His roommate beat the shit out of him," Sam said, and it sounded like he pulled out his keys. "Something about being a witch lover. I don't know. We just need to get to him. His teammates are trying to make him go to the hospital." He paused. "Josh, can you go with me?"

"Of course I can." Dad blew out a breath. "Emma, call us when you can. Go somewhere safe."

"I will." I still couldn't believe what had happened. "I'll call you tonight to check on him."

"Let's go, Sam," Dad said, and seconds later, I heard the door shut.

"Baby, please tell me you're safe." Mom's anxiety-riddled voice pulled at my heart even more.

"Yes, I am." If the Murphy pack was tracking us, the longer I stayed on this phone, the easier it would be for them to find us. "Mom, I've got to go. I'll call you tonight, okay?"

"Tell that boy if you two need anything, he better not hesitate to call," Mom said with vigor.

You better go. If Prescott beat Jacob up, they know we killed their pack members and got away. They'll be on the hunt. Aidan's jaw clenched with anger.

"Okay, I love you." I ended the call before I could somehow make things worse. I rolled down the window and threw my phone out of the car. It hit the ground, shattered, and rolled under the wheel of Coral's car.

"What happened?" Amethyst leaned forward and caught my eye.

"Prescott beat up Jacob." The Hallowed Guild would hurt every single person I cared about. "This has to stop."

"Oh, no," Beatrice rasped. "The Jones pack must have realized their scouts are all dead."

"Yeah." I ran a hand down my face. "But what's worse, I didn't even think about him." It never crossed my mind that they might hurt him. I mean, why the hell would they?

"He was at college, and Prescott is part of the football

team." Aidan's jaw clenched. "There was no reason for you to worry. I'm surprised he did it too."

"Look, bad things happen." Beatrice pointed at me. "You aren't to blame and shouldn't feel responsible. You didn't ask for that mark or a life like this. You were chosen. It's okay to feel hurt and pain over those who get hurt or worse along the way, but you can't beat yourself up about it."

Those words resonated deep within me. Hell, it had to be my wolf or witch part that understood because my human mind wasn't all that deep.

"She's right." Amethyst gave me a sad smile. "But no matter what, we're here for you."

And that was the only thing that would get me through.

We reached the witches' home right around lunch. The place had about fifty houses just like the last, but they were bigger. This neighborhood was out in an urban area with thick woods surrounding it. Despite them not having lived here for a while, the houses seemed in good shape, probably due to the all-brick exteriors.

Once again, we split up into houses. Aidan and I were staying with Beatrice and Amethyst in a large ranch. They gave us our own room at the back of a house overlooking the woods. We could easily slip out the window and run if we so desired.

This room was twice the size of the one back at the mountain. It held a large king-sized bed in the center, with a chest of drawers on one wall, and nightstands on either side of the bed. The floor was a light yellow hardwood, and the sheets were forest green, making the room feel earthy.

"Come on." Aidan locked the door, crawled into bed, and patted the spot next to him.

He didn't have to ask twice. I joined him on the bed, but surprisingly, sleep wasn't on my mind. I scooted over to him and placed my lips on his.

He responded in earnest and pulled me against him. *Damn, I missed this.*

I smiled despite us kissing. *It was just last night.*

Too damn long. His tone was dead serious.

My body warmed at his touch, and I needed more of him now. I slipped my hand under his shirt and enjoyed the warm buzzing that increased my need.

He growled as he pulled the shirt over his head, and then he pulled me on top of him. *You're driving me crazy.*

Good. I kissed down his jaw to his neck, enjoying his musky scent and taste.

His hands dug into my hips before grabbing the bottom of my shirt. *Off now.*

A giggle escaped me as I let him yank it over my head. Just as I tried to lean back over, he shook his head and unfastened my bra.

I removed it from my shoulders and flung it to the ground.

His golden eyes darkened, drinking me in. *Now we're on to something.* He rolled me onto my back and leaned over me. He removed my jeans and underwear and shimmied out of his.

As soon as we were naked, he lay beside me and lowered his head to my breasts.

When his mouth touched my nipple, my breath caught. His tongue began working, and my breathing became rapid. *Aidan.*

Damn, I love hearing you say my name. His hand slowly traveled down and touched between my legs.

No one had ever touched me like that before him, and when he began to rub, it was as if he knew the right place instinctively. He probably did. He was my mate, for God's sake.

His body did crazy things to mine, and the friction began to increase. *Please take me.* I needed him inside me.

He released my breast and positioned himself between my legs. As he guided himself to my entrance, he kissed my lips. *I love you.*

I love you too.

As soon as those words left my thoughts, he thrust inside me. We didn't have to start slow since it wasn't my first time.

Each movement brought us closer together despite us already having completed the bond. His lips captured mine, and his taste, smell, and sensations were heaven. Nothing had ever fit so perfectly or made so much sense to me.

If all that pain had been necessary to get us here, it had all been worth it.

Soon, waves of pleasure cascaded over us, and my body quivered with ecstasy. There couldn't be a drug better than him.

"You are fucking amazing." He kissed me as he rolled off and pulled me into his arms.

You're pretty amazing yourself. My eyes grew heavy, and I drifted off to sleep. It was scary how much I already depended on him to keep me safe. I only hoped I could return the favor.

CHAPTER FOUR

The sun came through the blinds, causing me to stir. I blinked a few times and snuggled closer to Aidan, enjoying waking up in his arms. His breathing was slow and steady, letting me know he hadn't woken yet.

The past few days had been god-awful, but I was the happiest I'd ever been. It had everything to do with the sexy-as-sin man lying right beside me and the friends I'd made at Crawford University.

I softly pressed my lips to his, morning breath be damned.

His eyelids fluttered. *Damn, I could get used to waking up like this.* His arms tightened around my waist.

Thanks for letting me know. I pulled back and grinned. *Can't have you getting spoiled.*

Hey now. He tickled my sides.

I giggled.

If you'd asked me three months ago if Aidan and I would be here in this moment, I would've said, "Hell, no." Maybe we'd needed to fall apart to be whole when the time came. I had no clue, but what we had now was stronger than ever before.

He rolled on top of me and grabbed my wrists, stretching them over my head. He smirked and lifted an eyebrow. "How should I punish you?"

"Whatever you do, don't kiss me." Yes, I totally wanted him to, but dammit, I had to at least pretend I didn't want him to.

"Oh, well then, that'll be it." As he leaned down, his hardness pressed against my thigh. "I'll have to inconvenience myself greatly to teach you a lesson." His lips met mine, and between his scent and our kiss, my mind fogged.

Someone banged on the bedroom door, and I almost jumped out of my skin. "I can smell you two down the hall." Beth's voice was loud and obnoxious. "Get out here, or suffer the consequences. We have work to do."

He growled and arched an eyebrow at me. "She's bluffing."

There was another loud knock. "No, I'm not. Get your asses out here before I come in there."

Are you sure you're friends with her? He caught my eye.

Yes, I'm sure. I didn't think I'd ever smiled this much in such a short period of time. *So we probably need to behave.*

I was afraid you'd say that. He sighed dramatically and captured my lips one more time.

A huge smirk crossed my face as he licked my lips and sucked on my bottom lip.

Heat blasted through my body, and he bit down a little harder.

You like that, huh? His golden eyes glowed, revealing that his wolf surged forward.

The doorknob turned, but it wouldn't open.

"Did you really expect it to be unlocked?" Surely she knew better.

"No, but I figured I'd try before I went all-out." Humor was clear in her voice.

She's up to something. I rolled off the bed and got to my feet. "We're up. Give us five minutes."

"That's all you're getting," Beth grumbled. "I'll be back."

"You aren't as scary as the Terminator." Aidan winked.

"Oh, you haven't seen anything yet." She grabbed the doorknob and turned it again.

"He's kidding." I was going to smack him. *If she comes in here and sees you like that, I can't be held responsible for her reaction.* Before Beth realized what he was to me, she'd referred to him as 'the guy' in our composition class. I couldn't blame her. He was downright delectable.

He got out of bed and grabbed his jeans off the floor. *I'm not sure if I should be proud or upset that you don't really care if she saw me naked.*

Let's say I'd rather she doesn't, but if you antagonize her, you'll get what's coming. I shrugged, collected my clothes, and headed into the bathroom.

The bathroom here was huge. Now that we were here, it was obvious this was their home. It contained more furniture and a comforting feel. It wasn't as sterile.

The tan tiles complemented the maple sinks. There was a white-tiled shower with a tub right beside it. I turned on the water and scanned the area. There was already shampoo and soap inside, which surprised me, but then I remembered Amethyst had mentioned that the people who got here first would set up the houses for the rest of us. They must have done this.

A small closet to the right contained fluffy white towels.

I laid one on the granite countertop. I stepped into the shower and turned on the water.

Halfway through, I felt a tingle down my back and turned to find Aidan leaning against the doorframe, watching me. "Enjoying the show?"

"It's taking every ounce of self-control I have not to join you." His husky voice told me every one of his desires.

"Good thing I'm done." If he kept looking at me like that, Beth would see something that couldn't be unseen. I turned the water off and grabbed the towel.

I hurriedly dressed, knowing the others were waiting on us.

Once I was ready, I took Aidan's hand and tugged him to the kitchen.

The scent of bacon filled the air. "Something smells good."

"Well, you were almost too late." Beth grabbed some bacon from the middle of the rectangular table.

Our crew was in their usual spots, with Beatrice at the head of the table, Amethyst on one side, and Sage on the other. Rowan sat between Amethyst and her daughter, Coral. Beth took up the last spot at the end. Samuel sat next to his mother and adopted brother, Finn.

I made my way over to Finn and sat down. "I thought you were coming in after five minutes?"

"Well, yeah, but when I smelled that you two had cooled down back there, I figured you would be out soon." Beth tapped her nose. "It was clear as day what you two were leading up to."

She really didn't have any boundaries. I busied myself by grabbing some food before I died of embarrassment.

"Hey, be nice." Aidan pointed at her as he sat beside

me. "Do you really want us to give you hell when you find your own mate?"

"Fine," she grumbled and shoved a whole piece of bacon into her mouth.

"Hey, I'm jealous." Coral leaned back and grabbed her cup of coffee. "It's nice to find a hot man and get some frustration out."

Rowan turned to her daughter and frowned. "You do realize your mother is sitting right here?"

"Mom, don't act all virginal." Coral motioned at herself. "You have a kid, remember."

"As fun as this conversation is, I think there are more important matters we need to discuss," Beatrice said. She fidgeted in her seat, clearly not comfortable with where the conversation had ventured.

Finn glowered at Aidan. "I have to agree with that."

Okay, this had to end before those two got into it again. "So ... my powers are unlocked, kind of."

"What do you mean, 'kind of'?" Samuel took a bite of his eggs, his eyes staying on me.

I reached over, took a biscuit, and shoveled some eggs and bacon onto it. "It's weird. There is this place inside me that was a dark void all my life. Now, it seems almost iridescent, but I still can't access it."

Aidan grabbed the coffee pot at the center of the table. "Here, want coffee?"

"Yes, please." I liked him taking care of me, which was strange. With Jacob, it had pissed me off.

"I've been thinking about that, and there is only one thing that Sage and I could come up with." Beatrice tapped the table.

Amethyst narrowed her eyes and tilted her head. "What's that?"

Sage turned her green eyes directly on me. "What did the two of you do right before the earthquake?"

I wished I could turn invisible.

"We claimed each other and completed the bond," Aidan said and took my hand.

Okay, he'd said it a lot more eloquently than I would've. My words would've been, "We did it," or "We had sex."

"That's what we thought. The two of you completing your bond released your powers." Beatrice let out a long sigh. "And from what I remember, the other girls are now marked too."

"They weren't marked before?" That didn't make any sense. Why would I be marked but not them?

"Because you were the catalyst, the chosen wolf to release them all."

"So that's why my forefathers never found more than one." Aidan scratched his neck.

Amethyst's brows furrowed. "Did you guys know to look for more than one?"

"No, but at the same time we—I mean, The Hallowed Guild doesn't trust witches, so they're always on the lookout for someone with the mark." His shoulders sagged, but he snatched a handful of bacon.

"'We,' huh?" Finn arched an eyebrow and faced Aidan.

Emma, I'm trying to get along with this asshole for you, but he keeps acting like this. Aidan's voice was full of rage despite his mask of indifference. *If he doesn't stop, I'll have to kick his ass. My wolf is ready to attack him right now.*

You're right. I thought he'd have calmed down by now, but he hasn't.

"Stop it," I said and moved my head so Aidan wasn't in his line of vision anymore. "He hasn't been part of them for about a week, so the word *we* was out of habit."

Finn's jaw clenched. "Exactly. He could turn any second."

"Oh, stop it," Beth said as she grabbed a biscuit and hurled it right at Finn. It hit him on the cheek and left some crumbs in his scruff. "He's locked and bound to Emma, so stop being an ass."

"I'm not too fond of you either, *wolf*." His contempt rang through the room.

"Well, you better get used to having us around." I hated his attitude, though I understood some of it. Being an orphan was hard even if you were raised by people who loved you. A piece of you would always be missing. Did I look like my parents? Did I have their laugh? Hell, would they be proud of me?

"She's right." Coral bit her fingernail. "You better get on board because there'll be more than those three around once we've rounded up the other girls."

"How many girls are there? You mentioned five sides." If I were a betting woman, I'd say four, but if I'd learned anything this past week, it was that I usually found out something new.

"Four." Beatrice smiled. "That much I remember. There are five points to a star, and thus each girl will represent a vertex."

"That's neat." Beth grinned and leaned back in her seat.

"Where are they?" I had no clue where to even begin the search. Honestly, I was waiting to wake up from this dream. Witches couldn't have babies with shifters unless it was time for a marked girl to be born. It sounded crazy. And the worst part was, if the witches birthed the hybrid, they didn't survive.

"From what I can remember of the prophecy, they are

all in the United States." Amethyst leaned over her mom. "It's so amazing to actually be part of this."

"I had no clue about any of this, but I'm not going anywhere." Beth straightened her shoulders. "There's no getting rid of me."

"It's strange how you guys think of it as a prophecy, but my dad thinks of it as a curse." Aidan chewed on a piece of bacon.

"Perception is important," Rowan stated. "The Hallowed Guild thinks having a female leader is the end of times while we believe an all-women council that brings witches and wolves together is a sign of progression and stability."

"That makes sense." Aidan sighed. "But how do we get them to realize it's not a bad thing?"

"You can't." Finn's face turned unreadable. "Those assholes don't care about anything other than themselves. They enjoy the fear they bestow upon us."

"I'm not sure I'd go that far, but Finn is right." Coral licked her lips. "That's why we need to create some sort of council. It's the only way to unify us. The wolves will fight it tooth and nail."

"Ha, love the pun." Beth chuckled.

Coral's forehead lined. "What pun?"

"You know what? Forget it." Beth waved her off.

"Okay ... so, the girls. How the hell do I find them?" It was all fun and games to talk about what we were going to do, but we were missing the first huge piece—finding them.

"That's one reason it's a good thing we're here." Beatrice picked up her napkin and dabbed her mouth. "We have a community building that contains all our spell books and history."

"So one of those books will tell us the whole story?"

Aidan's shoulders relaxed as if he'd expected it all to be harder.

"Yes, it does," Beatrice said, wincing.

"Great, let's go get it." Beth stood and motioned for everyone to get up.

"There is a slight problem." Sage stared us down. "We aren't sure which one it is."

"That's no big deal." It didn't seem as bad as she was making it out to be. "Let's go look through them."

"When we say 'history books,' we're talking about thousands." Rowan sighed. "When we got here, we put our things away, but we didn't have time to organize or anything. We'll have to find the answers as we get the library in order. It'll take a minute."

Of course it would. Nothing could ever be so simple. "Then, I guess we'd better get to work. We need to find those girls before The Hallowed Guild does." Hopefully, fate was on our side and we would find the information quickly. Otherwise, we might find out what happened when the chosen wolf didn't finish her job.

CHAPTER FIVE

The next week passed in a blur. We spent all of our time, opening box after box, looking for the book that contained the prophecy. When Beatrice had mentioned they needed to put the library together, she hadn't been exaggerating.

There were so many damn books.

And the topics varied widely—everything from healing spells, to hexing spells, to Mother Nature, to potions. I spotted something with the word *death* on it, and I quickly ran away from that. I didn't need any more bad juju around me.

But the most amazing thing happened in the least expected way—I finally didn't feel so alone anymore. I wasn't sure if it was from being around the witches or bonding with my mate—hell, maybe it was a combination of the two—but I felt like I belonged somewhere for the first time in my life.

"I'm going cross-eyed." Beth stood from the dark cherry wood table. She glanced across the table at me and Aidan, then turned her head at Amethyst, who sat next to her. "How many books do we still have to go through?"

The library was a huge building in the middle of the coven's neighborhood. It was the same size as the other ranch-style homes, but it had huge bookshelves built into the walls, and there were at least five large tables in the center. The only other room in here was the bathroom in the corner.

"Are you really asking her that question?" I pointed to the twenty boxes left to go through. We'd already unpacked over three-fourths of the library, but it had taken our core group of ten working around the clock in shifts, and we hadn't found anything useful.

"You'd better be glad I love you." Beth pointed at me. "Because if I didn't, your ass would be getting a beat down."

Aidan growled beside me.

Beth narrowed her eyes at him. "Are you threatening to hit a girl?"

"You're threatening my mate, and you all want equal rights, so—" Aidan started.

"Okay, we're all tired and irritable." Amethyst lifted her hands in the air. "Beth, why don't you go back to the house and rest for a little while?"

"None of you are leaving." Beth pouted.

"You were here before us." Beth had been here nonstop, even more so than Aidan and me. In all fairness, I was surprised she hadn't gotten stressed like this before now. "So go. We'll be switching off with Finn and Samuel in about an hour."

"Look, I'm sorry." She ran a hand down her face. "Mom called me this morning, and we got into a huge argument."

"Are you fucking serious?" Aidan slammed his hand on

the table and glared at her. "Why the hell didn't you toss your phone?"

Beth blinked a few times. "I wasn't part of the pack …"

"But they know you were Emma's roommate and that you're with her now." Aidan stood and held his hand out. "Give me your phone. We need to get rid of it."

Crap, I hadn't even thought about it. "Aidan, it's not her fault. Calm down." I touched his arm, using our mate bond to calm him. I glanced at Beth. "But he's right." I winced. I hated that I was tearing up everyone's lives. "We need to get rid of your phone."

"Yeah, we do." Beth ignored Aidan's outstretched hand. Instead, she placed her phone on the ground and stood. Then, she lifted her leg and stomped on it several times.

"We can share my burner phone for parental calls." I forced a smile even though it turned my stomach. I was ready for this whole thing to be over, but it was only beginning.

Aidan looked at Amethyst. "We need to have people on alert."

"I'll text Mom." Amethyst picked up her phone and typed out a message.

It hadn't been ideal for Beth to call her mom on her phone, but she had and was upset over it. She deserved a friend right now. It was clear she was a good one to me. "What did you two argue about? Not being on campus?"

"The school called her since I hadn't been in class for a week. They went by our dorm and found us gone." Beth rolled her eyes. "So she called me in a panic, demanding to know where I was."

"You didn't tell her, right?" Aidan's body somehow tensed even more. "For all we know, Prescott or someone else from the pack could've contacted your mom."

"Of course not, which made it all worse." Beth sat back down and crossed her arms. "I told her there was something important going on and she had to trust me."

I hated to do it, but it was my responsibility to lay it out for her. "If you go back, they'll hurt you or worse." I felt like a horrible friend for having dragged her into this. "I'm sorry, but Bradley and Prescott know all about you. If something were to happen ..." I trailed off, not wanting to think about it.

"Don't worry." Beth reached across the table and touched my hand. "I won't leave you. You're my best friend, and you need everyone you can get in your corner." She lifted her hand off mine and waved. "It's not like I can't go back to college when this is all over."

"I know, but I hate what I've done to everyone." It wasn't just Beth who'd left Crawford midway through a semester. We all had. "Not only that, but you all put yourselves behind on your graduation."

"It's an honor for us." Amethyst placed a hand on her heart. "The prophecy is told to every single witch as a child. You're a beacon of hope for a safe future—one where we won't have to worry if the wolf pack next door hates us."

Yeah, that wasn't much pressure or anything. "But you were in college."

"Have you ever considered how our coven operates?" Amethyst reached across the table. "How we can live and stay hidden for the most part?"

"Actually, no. I haven't." That was a good question.

"It's because we do most of our work and business over the internet. One coven member does bookkeeping. Another is a lawyer who works from the base. We each have a job we perform from home. That's the beauty of the internet these days." Amethyst stretched her arms. "Honestly, they expected us to do college over the internet, but the four of us went against the grain. The university tugged at us. Now, we know why."

"That's so strange because, the day we met six years ago, I was tugged to the line where the prettiest girl I'd ever seen was standing." Aidan's eyes filled with adoration as he looked at me.

"Well, that's because she's your fated mate, dumbass." A proud smile spread on Beth's face.

Aidan glared at her.

She needed to tread lightly. He wasn't in a humorous mood.

I kissed him. "Ignore her. She's just jealous."

Amethyst giggled. "You guys are so much fun, but I get Aidan's point. I believe we were drawn to you since your mom was a member of this coven. You couldn't stumble upon the coven, so the Goddess brought us to you."

"Like meeting in the middle." That made sense, but I wasn't sure how to live up to everyone's expectations. What if I failed? That wasn't an option, but I couldn't stop the horrible thoughts from invading my mind.

"Fate is one manipulative bitch." Beth snorted. "Remind me never to get on her wrong side."

"Or we could say fate knows how to make things work out." Amethyst nodded. "That's how witches think."

"They pretty much mean the same thing, don't they?" Aidan chuckled.

"Yeah, yeah." I stood and headed over to the boxes we still had to sort through. I opened a box and scanned the contents. The books in here were older than the others, which was what we were looking for.

Something tugged me ... called me. My hands were drawn to something deep inside.

I moved the books around gently, doing my best not to mess up the old bindings barely holding the various books together.

For some reason, I knew the exact book I needed to get my hands on even though I had no clue what it looked like. Finally, my hand touched old leather. It felt more worn. Deep wrinkles marred the smooth material.

What's that? Aidan pulled out a book and left it on the table.

He must have felt my confusion through our bond. *I'm not sure.* I gingerly pulled the book out. It looked either really old or like it had suffered some hard times. Hell, it could've been both. *I was drawn to it.* The spine didn't have a title or anything, unlike all the other books.

What was most shocking was the magic radiating from it. It latched onto my skin and headed toward the iridescent magic still chained inside me.

"Did you find something?" Amethyst asked, her eyes on the box.

I placed the book on the table, and Amethyst inhaled sharply.

"That's it." She stood and hurried over to my side. "I remember that binding from my childhood." She grabbed her cell phone and typed out a message.

Beth wrinkled her nose. "It smells like musty leather."

"That's exactly what it is." I opened the book. The paper was yellow and so brittle it felt like it might disintegrate in my hand. "How old is this?"

"Well, the original witch lived hundreds of years ago, so there really is no telling." Amethyst shook her head. "Mom never let me open this when I was little. We had it in our old library back at Mount Juliet. We kept all our sacred books in a special place."

"I thought she'd cursed the alpha while she was in labor?" How did someone make a book like this while they were on their deathbed?

"She did, but she prepared this first. You see, when he found out she was pregnant, he refused to see her." Amethyst frowned. "So she started prepping."

Aidan's forehead creased. "Are you saying the witch planned to do this to the alpha?"

"How would you feel if someone you loved walked away from you, but not to protect you?" Beth lifted an eyebrow at him. "Instead, it was because she was a woman and worthless? He didn't love her or her child."

"Look, we aren't here to fight about whether the witch was justified." Rehashing the past wouldn't change a damn thing. "We're here to understand what is expected so that no one else has to die and witches and wolves can get along."

"She's right." Amethyst slowly turned the page, and writing came into view.

The words were clear. "It says that when she told the alpha she was pregnant, he tried to kill her on the spot."

"Wait ... you can read that?" Aidan's forehead was lined with confusion.

"Yes, it's in English." It didn't sound like he was trying to be funny, but the question was so odd. Now wasn't the time for jokes.

"No, it's not." He scooted his chair closer. "It's like symbols or something. It looks similar to Chinese."

"Really?" He had to be messing with me.

"He's right, Emma." Beth looked at me. "Are you messing with us?"

"No, it's because we're direct descendants of her

coven." Amethyst's eyes brightened. "I heard that powerful witches could do that."

The front door opened, and Beatrice, Sage, Rowan, and Finn entered the room.

They hurried over, and when Beatrice's eyes landed on the book, they widened.

"You found it." Beatrice made her way between Amethyst and Beth. She touched the book. "When we were getting out of Mount Juliet, some of the younger coven members packed up the library. They didn't mark which box contained the oldest books, not knowing any better."

"It's amazing. I've never been this close to it." Rowan touched the book.

"Why haven't you been this close?" If the book was that important to them, it surprised me that she hadn't seen it until now.

"Because these books are so old we try not to touch them." Sage nodded at them. "That's the best way to preserve them."

Beatrice gingerly turned the pages as she scanned the words. "How to find the others is near the back."

"Maybe the full-blooded wolves should leave the room." Finn frowned as he glanced from Beth to Aidan.

He had to stop this shit. "No, they're staying. They are just as involved as the rest of us." I dared him to disagree.

It shocked me when he kept his mouth shut.

I love you. Aidan's voice filled my head.

I watched Beatrice inspect the pages toward the back. "It's huge for just a curse, though." I mean the curse sounded complicated, but not like two-hundred-pages complicated.

"This was her diary throughout her pregnancy. It really isn't much more than her heartbreak and lack of understanding. Each time she tried to talk to the Murphy Alpha, he punished her." Beatrice kept flipping through the pages.

"Punished her?" That sounded extreme. "How?"

"One time, he killed a rabbit and hung it from a tree outside her house." Beatrice grimaced. "Another time, he had pack members sneak in and destroy her garden."

"Did the Rogers pack do nothing about it?" Beth asked.

"That's what made our packs enemies." Aidan huffed and took my hand. "We were close until this whole thing went down."

"So you guys didn't hate us until then?" Finn's usual animosity was gone, which was strange.

"No, we didn't accept them like the Rogers pack did, but we didn't actively dislike them." Aidan shrugged. "At least, according to the story."

"This is when she made the curse." Beatrice turned the book to face us. Instead of the neat handwriting from before, this was messy and almost illegible. "This is when he left her before the baby was born. She talks about a girl being the catalyst of the alpha male's demise. That if she came into her powers, there would be a girl to represent each piece of the star and together they would bring the supernaturals together in the new world."

"So, five." Beth nodded. "That makes sense. But a new world?"

"Yes, that's what the witches called the United States then." Beatrice flipped to the back of the book. "But this part has always puzzled me."

"Blank pages." Aidan touched the paper with his free hand. "Did she die before she could finish it?"

"No, it says only the blood of the star can guide you to the next, and when it's complete, the women will be able to see beyond, once they've proven they are worthy." She pointed to the last words written on the previous page.

"Great, so I have to find the girls, and then we bleed on here." A witch set this into motion, so I shouldn't have been surprised. During my short stay here, I'd learned that blood was one of the most powerful ingredients in any spell.

Rowan's eyes lit up. "I can't believe we get to be part of this."

"And it sounds like that's how you find the next marked girl." Amethyst bit her bottom lip and raced over to the section of maps we'd put up the other day. She grabbed one of the United States and hurried back over to us.

"Yes, it does." Beatrice moved the book off the table and motioned to the ones in front of Beth and Aidan. "Move them out of the way. I don't want to risk ruining them."

Aidan and Beth moved the books to the table next to us as Amethyst spread out the map.

"Okay, we can try it and see what happens." Beatrice nodded in my direction. "Can you find something to prick your finger and drip blood on the map? Then, we'll do a locator spell. If what the book says is correct, it should work."

Aidan stiffened beside me and whispered, "Are you sure about this?"

"Are you expecting us to use her blood for something else?" Finn sneered. "After all this, you don't trust us."

"That's not what I meant," Aidan growled and stood. "Remember that conversation we had a few days ago? It's still relevant, you know."

"Then, why don't we take this outside." Finn wiggled his fingers. "I'm ready for a fight."

Dear God. I wasn't sure what the hell I needed to do to get him to quit acting like this, but he was pissing me off.

"You will stop being ornery." Sage pointed at Finn and chastised him. "You're always trying to pick a fight with him. If you want one, I'll gladly remind you who is in charge of my household."

Finn's face turned a shade of pink.

We had more important things at hand than male egos. "It doesn't hurt to try." I put my finger in my mouth and bit down on my fingertip. I pulled it out as blood welled. "Where do I put it?" I had no clue what I was doing.

"Drip the blood anywhere, and it should move to where your target is." Amethyst gave me a comforting smile. "Trust your witch side to know what to do."

Yeah, that probably wouldn't work out well. "I'll try." I held my hand over the map. *I won't lie. I feel stupid.*

Aidan chuckled through our bond. *You're fine. I'm just not thrilled about you dripping your blood everywhere. I mean, I know you trust these witches, but ...*

What other option do we have? And honestly, I feel connected to them. I got that he was hesitant because of how he was raised, but it was time for him to get over it. I trusted them. I turned my finger over and five drops of blood landed in the center of the map. Amethyst's and Beatrice's hands hovered over the map as they quietly chanted.

It was creepy. The blood crept to the right, heading toward the Virginias. It inched over West Virginia and settled on a small city named Clarksburg.

"Holy shit. That was strange as hell." Beth froze as if she couldn't believe what she saw.

"Magic is always surreal when you are first around it," Amethyst said as she patted Beth on the shoulder. "But do you realize what this means? We now know where the first girl is."

"Then, we need to get there." We'd lost a week, which was a big deal with The Hallowed Guild searching for us.

"It's almost eight p.m." Aidan picked up his new phone from the table and pulled up a map. "And Clarksburg is ten and a half hours away. We need to rest and head out there first thing in the morning."

He was right, but I hated waiting another day. "Okay, bright and early."

"That works for me." Beth grinned.

"You should stay here where it's safe." I didn't want anyone else getting hurt. Aidan would demand to go, and honestly, I wouldn't fight him. I needed him with me.

"Nope, I'm in this with you." Beth winked. "Where you go I go until this whole thing is over."

"Okay." Even if I didn't like it, she was a grown-up and could make her own decisions. "Then, let's get back and get ready."

Tomorrow, I would begin the journey fate had planned for me so long ago.

CHAPTER SIX

Aidan

I woke up to a cold, empty bed. I glanced around, looking for Emma, but she wasn't in the room. Fear coiled inside me. *Emma?*

Yeah?

Hearing her voice calmed my racing heart. *Where are you?*

I'm outside. She sighed through our bond. *I needed a run.*

The clock glowed midnight. *You're out there all alone.* I jumped to my feet and climbed through the window. Yes, we should be safe here, but until all of this was over, I felt the need to be with her at all times—so I could keep her safe.

I'm fine, she tried to reassure me. *I'll be back in a few minutes.*

No, I want to go with you. The last time we'd been in wolf form, we'd fought Prescott's pack. A run did sound nice. *Where are you?*

I just shifted. She laughed. *I tried to be sneaky.*

See, you can never get away from me. I tried keeping this light because I felt how much she was struggling. She didn't realize how damn strong she was, and I felt her fear almost constantly. That was one of the things I loved about her—she cared so much. She didn't want to disappoint anyone.

I saw her pajamas on the ground, so I stripped down and placed mine next to hers. I let my wolf surge forward, and soon, I was on four feet. I caught her scent and raced toward her.

Her blonde wolf waited for me several feet inside the woods. Her gray eyes were dark. I hated that she carried this burden on her shoulders. *You know, we could run away.* I'd been thinking about it more and more lately. Yes, she might have activated the other girls, but who said she had to fulfill the prophecy? We could leave the United States and live somewhere else. She deserved to be free … to be happy … to have a chance at a life without fear.

Emma

THE FACT that Aidan was willing to run away with me meant so much. He was all in—as if I'd needed further proof. *As nice as that sounds, we can't do that.*

Why not? His dark wolf trotted over to me, and he rubbed his face against my neck.

Because if I can stop the killing and mistreatment, then I need to stay. It'd be so easy to run away, but I would never forgive myself if I did. It would be the simple path and not the one I needed to take.

Can't blame me for trying. His golden eyes shone

brightly in the moonlight. *I just want you safe, happy, and taken care of.*

It was crazy how quickly our relationship had changed. I understood now why he had disappeared, especially since I was in a similar role. I'd do everything possible to keep him and the rest of my family safe, which included the witches. *And I want you to be safe too ... so maybe you can stay back while I go look for the girls.*

Uh ... hell, no. His tone was stern.

I stuck my tongue out at him, which didn't work quite as well in wolf form. I used the words he'd only just said moments ago. *Can't blame me for trying.*

Then, we took off running under the full moon.

AIDAN GRABBED the bag I'd packed for us off the bed and opened the bedroom door.

"Are you ready to grab something to eat and hit the road?" Aidan pressed his lips to mine.

"The longer we take, the more likely it is that The Hallowed Guild will find the girls." Which meant we needed to get moving and fast. "So, yep, let's get on the road."

We walked down the hall to the living room and found four other bags near the door. I wasn't sure why there were so many. Did Beth really need four bags' worth of clothes?

"Emma?" Beth called from the kitchen. "Everybody's ready to roll, and I packed you some breakfast."

"Everybody?" I took Aidan's hand and glanced into the kitchen.

"Hell, yeah." Samuel entered the living room and lifted what had to be biscuits wrapped in aluminum foil. "How do you expect to get all the girls back and deal with the covens you'll be staying with?"

I hadn't planned on getting the local covens to help. The last thing I wanted was to put other covens at risk. "We'll figure it out as we go." I didn't want to pull them away from their lives more than I already had. It didn't seem right.

"You'll need my help." Amethyst pointed at Coral and Samuel. "And it wouldn't hurt to have some backup. Make the witches feel better about ... uh ... you guys."

"You mean wolves." Aidan's voice was hard but factual. "I take it you're expecting the covens to shut us out."

Beatrice entered the room with a cup of coffee. "I'm expecting you all to head into areas where The Hallowed Guild might be located."

"Why would you say that?" It didn't make any sense. Aidan had mentioned there were only a handful of branches throughout the United States. Why would Beatrice presume The Hallowed Guild would be located near each of the marked girls?

Sage joined us in the room and stood next to Beatrice.

Sage ran her hands through her hair. "Because the Guild split off into areas they suspected marked girls might be. The other books that were with the original witch's diary document the last four girls who were born with the mark. We'll be doing some research after you go. Hopefully, we can find some helpful information."

The front door swung open, and loud footsteps pounded toward us. His auburn hair was messy as if he'd woken up moments ago, and his clothes were wrinkled.

Finn focused on Samuel, and his face was set in a deep scowl. "You turned off my alarm so I'd oversleep?"

Sage scolded her son. "You were supposed to tell him he wasn't going."

"I thought it'd be easier if he woke up after we'd left." Samuel grimaced.

"Are you fucking kidding me?" Finn's jaw clenched as he glared at Beatrice. "Is this your doing?"

"Young man, you better watch yourself." Beatrice jabbed a finger in his direction and then glowered at Samuel. "You were supposed to handle this last night."

Samuel averted his gaze to the wooden floor, not meeting anyone's eyes.

Coral had her own food in her hand as she entered the room with her mother next to her.

Coral motioned to Finn. "Are you really surprised? Look at how you're acting."

"Me?" Finn shook his head, staring at them in confusion. "You guys are acting like life is normal."

No one wanted to set him right, and he was getting worse. I hated to do this since he was my cousin, but enough was enough. "You're irrational and full of hate."

"Excuse me?" He focused on me, and he pouted. "You don't even know me."

"I don't have to know you to feel it." I stared my cousin down. "You want to point fingers at Aidan, Beth—hell, even me—but we aren't the problem."

Emma, are you sure this is the time? Aidan squeezed my hand, and concern flowed through our bond.

If not now, when? I had to stick to my guns, and my gut was telling me this was long overdue. "You're an orphan, and it sucks."

"What the fuck does that have to do with anything?" His breathing increased, and if he could have, he'd have been spewing flames right now; that's how furious he was.

"Everything." I let go of Aidan's hand and stepped toward him. "I understand what you're feeling, but I handled it differently. I was afraid to upset people because it might make them not want me. My method wasn't healthy, and neither is yours."

"Oh, so you're psychoanalyzing me now?" Finn asked, his voice raspy.

"Maybe. You're doing the same thing but with anger. Instead of pleasing, you push your hate on everyone else." Now that my words were flowing, there was no stopping them. "You're a liability, and you need to learn to accept yourself. Until then, you'll hate and alienate yourself even more from the people you do care about."

"I'm not the one who killed my parents," he said so loud it hurt my ears.

"And neither did they." I pointed to Beth and Aidan. "What happened was tragic, but at least you knew your parents. I only found out who mine were weeks ago."

"So your story is sadder than mine?" Finn laughed, without humor. "I just need to shut up and be happy since I have a picture of them and you never did of yours?"

That hurt. I had no clue why, but it did.

Aidan growled, sensing my feelings, and moved to step in front of me, but I countered.

No one was fighting my battles for me.

"It's not a fucking competition." My wolf rose inside me, not giving a damn if it pissed him off more. "And that's your problem. Aidan was raised by the Society. You can't blame him for that. He's on our side now, and Beth has been nothing but kind to you. You need to do some soul-searching and get your act together."

"I should be part of this," he murmured. "My parents died protecting your mom."

"Maybe, but you're too hot-headed, and I don't want you with us." I hated to hurt him. This was important to him, but I couldn't risk him messing everything up. If we ran into The Hallowed Guild, I didn't need a loose cannon on my side. "I can't trust you to keep a level head."

He inhaled sharply and glanced at Beatrice, then Rowan, then Sage. "And you agree with her?"

"Yes, we do." Beatrice nodded, but her light purple eyes darkened with sadness. "You're getting worse each year."

"Fine." He turned on his heel and headed out the door, slamming it loudly behind him.

Tears sprang in Amethyst's eyes. "He's crushed."

"Maybe this is the wake-up call he needs." Coral wrapped her arms around Amethyst and smiled.

"I'm sorry if I spoke out of place." I'd followed my gut, but maybe I should've let Beatrice handle that encounter.

"No, you did so much better than me." Beatrice's shoulders slumped. "I wouldn't have been so honest, and maybe that's what he needed all these years."

"So ... changing the subject, but if we're getting four girls, and there are six of us, how many vehicles are we taking?" Beth held out her hands as she counted.

"We've got two Suburbans out there." Samuel nodded to the front door. "That way, none of us will be squashed."

"I'm riding with Aidan and Emma," Beth called out.

"Of course, the wolves would stick together." Coral winked at us.

"Here you go." Samuel tossed the keys at me.

"Uh ... I don't drive huge-ass vehicles." In fact, I had a hard time driving my dad's Nissan Altima back home.

"I've got this." Aidan grabbed the keys from me. "Let's roll."

It was around eight p.m. when we rolled into Clarksburg, West Virginia. We'd barely made any stops and got there within twelve hours.

We followed Samuel's SUV as he led us toward the local coven. Beatrice had made the call personally, and the local coven had invited us to stay. However, Coral had informed us that they might be wary. Whatever the hell that meant.

We were about twenty miles from the city, and I was afraid we might be on a wild goose chase. Maybe they'd given Beatrice incorrect information or something.

"Do you think we'll ever get out of here?" Beth yawned in the back middle row and raised her arms over her head.

"Not at this rate," I muttered. My legs were cramped, and my back hurt from sitting in this car all day. The fact that I sounded like an old woman pissed me off even more.

"Beatrice's coven is this far away from the city too." Aidan rubbed his thumb along my wrist. "It's just that you've been in the car all day and are eager to get out."

Yeah, my wolf didn't enjoy it at all.

Samuel slowed down and turned onto a small side road.

I was getting excited. This had to be a sign that we were getting close to our destination.

"Are we sure these witches will let us in there?" Beth leaned forward in the seat.

Anxiety threatened to take over, but I was keeping it at bay. "I'm sure it'll be fine." I tried sounding confident.

Nothing will happen to you. Aidan squeezed my hand again. *I won't allow it.*

I doubt they'll ask for your permission. I loved that he

was trying to comfort me. I would be a complete mess without him by my side.

Doesn't matter. He looked at me with love in his eyes.

We turned down a gravel road, and the SUV bounced from side to side.

"I thought we wouldn't be jarred around in this huge-ass car," Beth grumbled in the back. "I'm so ready to get out of it."

"Gravel isn't even, and the Suburban isn't magical. It won't be smooth the entire time." Aidan rolled his eyes and grinned.

"What the hell is that up there?" I squinted through the dust the lead vehicle was kicking up. A group of twenty people was blocking the road ahead.

The brake lights of the Suburban in front of us lit up, and as Samuel slowed, my cell phone went off.

I grabbed it from the center console and read the message. **Stay in until we motion for you to get out.**

"What does it say?" Aidan glanced at me.

"We're supposed to stay put." My heart began to race. That couldn't be a good sign.

CHAPTER SEVEN

My eyes focused on the four witches who stood in front of the other sixteen, blocking our way into their neighborhood. The place still wasn't in sight, so they didn't want us to get too close until they'd vetted us.

An unsettling feeling pulsed through me as I scanned our surroundings, looking for any sort of threat.

Are you okay? Aidan linked with me, and I noticed his body was even more tense. I didn't see how that was possible.

"I'm not one to be paranoid around witches, but damn." Beth shook her head.

"All right, I'm not waiting any longer." It'd only been a few minutes, but even Samuel, who was usually happy-go-lucky, seemed concerned from where we sat. I wasn't leaving it up to them to fend for us.

"Emma ..." Aidan warned.

He didn't like me risking myself, but that was something he would have to get over.

I opened the car door, climbed out, and slammed the door behind me.

Coral turned around and glared at me.

Yeah, she wanted me to go away, but I was done taking orders—at least for now.

Two car doors shut behind me. Aidan and Beth had also gotten out of the car. I wasn't thrilled about that, but what could I do? They were following my lead.

Finally, we walked around the lead vehicle so the four witches came into view. Two women stood in the center.

The older one was to the left. She had long silver hair that reflected the moonlight. She also had crow's feet around her eyes, but there was something youthful about her skin. Her silver eyes landed on me. "You brought wolves."

I wasn't sure if it was more of a statement or disgust.

"Beatrice lied to us." The other woman jerked her head, making her black hair bounce. She was younger than the other witch, but not by much. Silver highlights streaked her hair, and Her black eyes turned to slits as she glowered at me.

"How so?" If they were trying to intimidate me, they'd need to try harder.

The two guys flanking the women scowled.

I blinked a few times, thinking I was seeing double. They had to be twins. The only difference was the one beside the darker-haired lady had longer mousy-brown hair than the other. They both crossed their arms, emphasizing how scrawny they were. They had to be in their mid-forties, and disgust filled their muddy-brown eyes. They looked down their noses at us.

I was pretty sure it was supposed to intimidate us, but it wasn't working.

"She said only coven members were coming." The older

woman's voice shook. "I knew something was up when she wouldn't be specific."

"I am a coven member." After all, my mom had been a member of their coven, and my energy matched theirs. I had even been inducted into their coven as an official member.

The other lady scowled at me. "You're a wolf."

There was only one thing I could do, and I hoped it wasn't a huge mistake. I made my way over to them, and Coral shook her head no.

The four of them stepped back.

Aidan linked with me, his anxiety clear through the bond. *Emma, I'm not sure this is smart.*

We don't have time to hem and haw. We couldn't be timid since time wasn't on our side. The longer it took to find those girls, the more likely one of them could die.

"See, you are planning on attacking us," the longer-haired guy said in a deep, raspy voice. He lifted his hands toward me. "I won't hesitate to retaliate."

"I'm not here to attack you." I turned my back to them.

"No, Emma," Samuel warned.

Ignoring him, I moved my hair to the side so the witches could see my mark.

"Is that ..." The dark-haired witch stumbled toward me. "No."

The older lady's forehead wrinkled. "But you're a wolf."

"I'm a hybrid." That was the first time I'd spoken those words out loud. Something inside me shifted as if a piece of me had locked into place ... acceptance.

"That means ..." The older lady placed a hand on her heart. "It really is happening."

"It is." Amethyst stepped beside me. "Mother didn't lie. We've accepted the wolves as one of us," she said, pointing to me, then Aidan, then Beth. "Aidan is her fated mate, and

Beth is her best friend. We need support from both the wolves and witches if she is going to survive."

The older lady nodded. "Fine. You're welcome to stay here, but know we're on high alert."

"How come?" Aidan took my hand in his.

"There is a wolf roaming around our neighborhood." She motioned to the houses. "That's the reason why the sixteen of us were out here. We needed to screen you all to make sure you were from Beatrice's clan and hadn't been compromised by our enemies. It made us even more nervous when no one got out of the second vehicle at first. We thought it might have been The Hallowed Guild trying to sneak in, and we were worried you might be compromised."

"No, we aren't." Amethyst nodded. "We were just protecting her. You never know when someone might switch sides."

I'd never seen Amethyst like this before. She was always so warm and caring. For the first time, I saw her as the Priestess she was to become, and she was good.

"I understand all too well." The older woman stepped aside with half the group following her, and the other woman stepped in the opposite direction with the rest of the group unblocking the road. "Please pull through. Stop at the first house on the left. That's where our guests stay."

"Okay." Amethyst nodded back to the Suburbans. "Let's go."

Aidan, Beth, and I were soon back in the car.

Aidan turned his eyes on me as he started the engine. "What would you have done if they didn't like what your birthmark represents?"

"Beatrice knew the woman." I had to downplay the risk I'd taken.

"Thirty years ago." Beth snorted. "I'm sure people can change in that time span."

"Exactly," Aidan growled, clearly not happy with me.

We pulled down the road, and after a quarter of a mile, the neighborhood finally appeared. It was smaller than Beatrice's and only had about twenty houses. I was surprised at the difference.

The houses were well-kept cabins. Each house had a garden in front with various herbs and plants growing. The woods surrounded their subdivision, keeping them hidden.

Aidan pulled up behind Samuel in the driveway of the house they'd instructed us to go to. We all got out of our cars, and I surveyed the tree line, making sure nothing seemed odd.

People stared out their windows at us. Samuel, Coral, and Amethyst probably couldn't see since the lights were off inside, but to my wolf eyes, they might as well have had their lights on.

Samuel followed my gaze. "Is everything okay?"

"Yeah, but a lot of people are watching us." It was strange, but I saw at least one person in each house.

"Well, covens aren't known to be super welcoming of outsiders." Coral cringed with annoyance. "So our presence has piqued their interest. How many are watching us?"

"Every house is." Aidan stepped in front of me as if he could shield me from them.

It was sweet but ridiculous. He needed my help to calm him so I placed a hand on his arm, which had his shoulders loosening and releasing part of his tension.

"So what do we do? Stand here and look pretty?" Beth raised her hands over her head, stretching again. "'Cause I'm exhausted."

"Wolves are notoriously impatient." The older lady chuckled behind us. "Some things never change."

"We've been on the road for over twelve hours." I glared at Beth and turned my attention to the four witches heading our way. "So please forgive us."

"There's nothing to forgive." The older lady held out her hand. "I'm Olive, the head priestess of the coven."

"Emma." I smiled and shook her hand. Something crackled between our palms, and I jerked back.

A low growl emanated from Aidan's throat. The two men surrounded Olive.

"What happened?" Beth glanced from me to the witch.

"I don't know." Was I losing my mind? "Did you feel that?"

"Feel what, dear?" Her forehead lined with worry.

"It was like a pop or sizzle when we touched." I was sure I hadn't imagined it. It didn't hurt, but I hadn't been expecting that.

Coral came over and patted me on the shoulder. "That's how witches can identify each other if they meet in places where they can't verbalize their connection. It's nothing to be alarmed about, and you only feel it the first time you touch."

"You've been a witch since you were a baby and didn't know that?" The darker-haired woman stepped forward and extended her hand.

"I just recently learned I'm a witch." I shook her hand, this time fully expecting the sizzle between us. I looked at my coven friends. "It didn't do that when I touched you when we first met." This didn't make sense.

"That's because your witch powers hadn't been uncovered," Amethyst explained.

"I'm Moon." She pointed to the man with shoulder-length hair. "And that's Jasper." She pointed to the other man. "And Jabbar."

I lifted my hand that held Aidan's. "This is Aidan, and that's my best friend, Beth."

"We're honored that you came here." Moon nodded at me.

"Let's get them inside and settled in." Olive waved us on as she pulled out a key from her dark green dress. She moved quickly for her age, and we were in the house within moments.

Inside, it took a minute for me to comprehend what I saw. The house appeared older on the outside, but inside, it was sleek and modern. The walls were painted a light brown, and it had an open floor plan so the kitchen and den were connected. There were two large couches as well as a loveseat and recliner with a painted brown coffee table in the center. There was a large flat-screen television over the stone fireplace.

"There are only three bedrooms, so hopefully that'll do." Olive winced when she looked across the room.

Samuel nodded. "Yeah, it's fine. I'll take the couch."

"And Amethyst and I can share a room," Coral said as she bumped her shoulder into Amethyst.

"Okay, good." Moon grinned.

"Will we meet the other coven members?" I was intrigued and wanted to meet everyone.

"Tomorrow." Olive took a few steps toward the door. "It's not safe to go out at night right now."

"Why not?" Aidan glanced out the window as if he was expecting a threat to appear.

"Because of the wolf stalking us that we already told you about." Jasper's voice was deep and no louder than a whisper.

"Is that normal?" Amethyst's purple eyes darkened.

"No, it's not." Olive sighed and glanced out the window. "It started recently. We can't figure out why. They also don't come together."

"Has anything happened to cause it?" This story tugged at me, but I wasn't sure why.

"Strangely enough, it was after that earthquake." Moon pursed her lips. "That in itself was unusual. There's no telling what kind of power was released."

"Why do you think it was power related?" And it was very interesting, this whole story. *Do you think those wolves might be The Hallowed Guild* keeping an eye on the witches?

Yeah, so we need to be careful. Aidan was so tense it had to be hard for him to move.

"There was no epicenter." Olive arched an eyebrow. "That's a sign of magic if there ever was one."

Unsure if we should tell her why, I decided to let my witchy friends own that decision.

"Well, times are different now." Amethyst caught my eye. "So ... there's no telling."

"We'll let you get settled." Olive motioned to the door. "Please make yourself at home. We will come by in the morning to introduce you to the others."

"Perfect." Amethyst smiled. "Thank you."

The four of them headed out the door, and when it shut, the room became silent.

I looked at Amethyst. "Why aren't we telling them everything?"

"There is a reason you're to unite the wolves and witches." Amethyst blew out a breath and gave me a smirk. "It's not just the two races."

"The divisions are within the races too." That was new news to me. "Wow, but you guys don't seem like enemies."

"We aren't, but we aren't allies either." Amethyst sat on the couch. "There's a lot of mistrust, so we treat each other with honor and respect and even help at times, but we aren't true friends."

"How come?" Beth frowned. "I thought witches bonded over nature and some shit."

"That's really beautiful, Beth." Coral snorted. "You speak so eloquently."

"Bite me," Beth growled.

"Do you think they might fight?" Samuel looked over at Aidan. "I'd love a good girl fight."

Aidan didn't bother to react. His attention was solely on the information at hand.

"The division started after the original witch. Her prophecy had the covens fighting over who was the strongest and should bear the savior. It was crazy. From what I've been told, witches were lining up to volunteer, or rather plead, to be the one, as if we could choose." Amethyst's forehead wrinkled. "It was preposterous to even consider we could decide where the marked ones were born."

"So then what?" There had to be more to the story.

"As we told you previously, there were several marked girls before you, each one born to a different coven, which fractured us further. It was a competition." Amethyst shrugged. "So now we all keep to ourselves and only help when needed or forced to. A witch would never turn down a request from another coven because then they would appear weak."

"But covens don't like asking for help because it also makes them look weak." Aidan huffed and ran a hand down his face. "Damn, you guys are more similar to wolves than you know."

"Most of us consider you a prophecy, and it's true. We were cursed just like the wolves by the original witch, and you're here to save us and make us whole." Amethyst placed her hands on her lap. "But how can we truly trust each other when our original mother turned her back on us?"

"She couldn't know this would happen ..." Beth glanced around the room. "Surely."

"She had the eye of foresight," Coral said. "She was the original witch and had all powers: foresight, magic, and heart. Since the bloodline is now diluted, only a handful of witches have even one type of strong magic beyond the spells each one of us can cast." She sat next to Amethyst and placed a hand on her arm. "She knew how her relationship with the alpha would end, but she foolishly thought she could change the outcome. In her anger, she damned us all. Now, it's up to you to put us all back together."

Her words made my stomach churn. I wasn't made for this. I'd thought the witches would have it together enough to help us, but it sounded like we were on our own.

A wolf howled close by, and something snapped inside me.

CHAPTER EIGHT

Aidan linked with me as he turned toward the window. *Emma, what's wrong? Get away from the window. It could be the Guild.*

I ... I don't know. I rushed to the window and was so thankful that this house was next to the woods. As I searched the area, a pair of glowing sky-blue eyes met mine. *But I feel something... a tug toward the wolf outside. I don't think she's the Guild.*

Amethyst ran over. Her breathing was rapid as if she sensed my concern and confusion. "What's out there?"

"A wolf." It might be one of the wolves the witches had mentioned. "I need to go outside."

"Dammit, no." Aidan took my arm. "That could be a Hallowed Guild member."

"It could be." He was right, but I couldn't ignore the tug. "But what if it isn't?" If that wolf was the girl we were looking for, we needed to help her before the other wolf found her.

"She's right." Beth nodded at me and headed over. "The wolf is trying to hide, for God's sake."

"Don't you think The Hallowed Guild would hide too?" Aidan lifted a hand. "They could be scouting the area, waiting on her."

"I've got to agree with Aidan on this." Samuel came over and started. "Those are some creepy, bright blue eyes."

"If it was the society, would they be staring us down while alone out there?" Coral hurried to the door. "If no one else is going to check it out, I will."

"Yes, they would if they knew who she was." Aidan frowned as he watched her touch the doorknob.

"We can't let her go out there alone." If he thought I would be okay with that, he'd lost his damn mind.

"I'll go with her." Beth sounded annoyed.

"Me too." Samuel headed to the door with her.

Aidan, we have to go with them. I tried not to be angry, but this was ridiculous. I got that he was trying to protect me, but we couldn't let others put themselves at risk without proper backup. *If what you said is true, others could be waiting to attack.*

His shoulders sagged as he gave in. *Fine, but you stay close to me. We stay back until we see how it all plays out.*

"We're going with you," I said and walked over to the others right when Coral opened the door.

"Well, I'm not the only one staying behind." Amethyst stood from the couch, and within seconds, the six of us were outside.

A low growl came from the trees the wolf hid behind.

"She's scared," Amethyst said quietly, but not quietly enough so the wolf couldn't hear.

A more threatening growl followed.

"Shh." I placed my finger to my lips. "She can hear you." At least we knew it was a girl now.

If she's scared, it isn't the Society. Out here, I felt a stronger pull toward her. I stepped toward the woods.

Emma, dammit. Aidan hurried next to me. *I said don't leave my side.*

I think she's the girl we're looking for. There was no other reason I'd feel drawn to her. I lifted my hands in front of me and took another slow and steady step. *Stay here.*

One wrong move, and I'm next to you in a flash. Aidan consented, even though unhappiness rang through our bond. His eyes glowed, but he reined his wolf back in.

That's fair. My focus was solely on her. I could only imagine what it would feel like to be alone in the woods after your magic had been uncovered. I was freaked out enough with Aidan, Beth, and the rest of the coven behind me.

She whimpered as if she was scared but couldn't leave.

I feel you. With each step, the tug got stronger and stronger.

I had to think about her and not my goal. Right now, I needed to connect with her. If I couldn't do that, there was no way in hell she'd leave with us.

Not sure what to say, I winged it. "I'm not here to hurt you." I made my voice soft but clear so she'd know I was talking to her.

Another whimper was her response.

This was inconvenient. She was in wolf form, and we weren't pack members. I could talk, but she couldn't respond, and if she was scared, she wouldn't shift back to human form.

"Look, nothing bad is going to happen." I stopped moving, not wanting to push my luck and cause her to run away. "I was hoping we could talk."

She responded with a low growl, which I'd expected.

Aidan and Beth hurried to my side. The wolf stepped away from us and farther back into the woods.

I glanced over my shoulder and held up my hand. *It's fine. Give me a few more minutes.*

Beth looked at Aidan, waiting for his reaction. "I'm assuming she's talking to you."

"Yeah, let's stay here." Aidan's golden eyes turned dark. *If she gets more aggressive, it's over.*

Okay. I scanned the woods and almost missed her. Her fur was as black as the night. Her eyes were my saving grace. "If we were going to hurt you, we would've tried by now."

Another howl came from close by. The girl froze and glimpsed behind her. Her gaze turned toward me one last time before she took off running.

"Shit!" I wanted to run after her, but that would likely scare her off for good. Whoever this second wolf was could not be her friend or pack member, not considering the way she'd reacted.

Emma, we need to get inside. Aidan linked with me as he ran over to me and grabbed my arm. He tugged me back to the house, making me stumble as I continued to search for her.

Branches cracked as the other wolf ran toward us. It wasn't easy to get my head on straight when she was gone and another wolf headed straight for us.

I spun around to face the house and motioned for the others to head inside. "Everyone hurry."

Whatever I did must have snapped Samuel, Coral, and Amethyst out of whatever fog they'd been in. Beth reached them, and the four of them got to the door in seconds.

Aidan and I were several feet behind. Even though we were wolves, we couldn't run as fast in human form.

Right when we were about to climb the stairs, the wolf ran out of the woods and charged directly at us.

We won't make it inside in time. I couldn't believe I'd been so fucking stupid. I might as well have handed myself over on a platter. Hell, those two wolves could have worked together and pretended to be enemies in order to get me out here, but I felt something with her, so it had to be a coincidence ... right?

Now wasn't the time to deal with this. I heard his paws dig into the ground, which told me he was lunging.

Aidan linked with me as he called his wolf forward. *Duck!*

His bones began to crack, and he pushed me hard.

I hit the ground, and pain radiated through my ass. Normally, I would've complained, but the wolf landed and stumbled where I'd been standing seconds ago.

I turned around to see Aidan in wolf form, his black fur reflecting the moonlight. He charged the almost white wolf as he tried to stand. Aidan lowered his head and steamrolled the wolf in the side, pinning it against a tree.

The wolf stood on two feet, extricating himself from Aidan's hold. As soon as he was back on four feet, he rose onto his hind legs and jumped on Aidan's back.

Oh, hell no. No one hurt my mate. I forced my shift, ripping through my clothes, desperate to kick some wolf ass. This asshole was going down.

The light-haired wolf's hazel eyes locked on my mate's neck.

If I didn't hurry, that's where he'd attack.

Aidan tried to buck him off like a bull in a rodeo. However, that wolf sank his claws into Aidan's side to hang on.

I pushed my legs as hard as possible and clamped down on the asshole's back leg.

The wolf whimpered in agony, and I jerked my head back, dragging him off my mate.

Emma, you're going to get hurt. Aidan's concern laced his words in my head.

Like you were. I needed him to realize we were a team and he wasn't my protector. I gnawed on the white wolf's leg as his claws unlatched from Aidan. He kicked his back leg, causing me to lose my grip, and knocked my feet out from underneath me. *We're a team—equals—get it through your damn head before you make me do something drastic.*

Our bond went silent.

Good. Maybe he would rethink how he was acting.

The light wolf turned toward me, baring his teeth.

Did he really think he could win with Aidan and me against him? As far as I could tell, he'd come alone. There were no red flags warning that others were coming to help him.

Right as he went in for the attack, Aidan jumped the wolf, and he crashed to the ground.

The front door opened, and Samuel and Beth ran out. Samuel grabbed a huge fallen tree branch and hit the wolf right in the head, knocking him out cold.

Beth motioned to the open door. "Go get changed. We'll deal with this."

Come on. Aidan ran toward the house. *We need to get back out here and question him before he gets away.*

Needing no further encouragement, I followed after him.

Aidan

As I led the way back to the bedroom, I tried to use the opportunity to calm myself down. Every time she put herself at risk, it drove me insane. She was my mate which meant I was supposed to protect her.

I wanted to yell and scream and tell her to stay out of harm's way, but I couldn't. I'd be no better than my father dictating what a mate should do. She deserved better than that. The original witch chose her, and if I stepped in the way, none of us might survive.

She was right even if I didn't like it. We had to work side by side, but damn, I didn't want to accept it.

Emma

After we'd gotten dressed, we headed back out to the living room. Amethyst and Coral were standing at the window, watching Samuel and Beth outside.

"He was scared too." Amethyst addressed us, but her eyes were focused on the window. "I don't think he was acting maliciously."

"But he attacked us when we were trying to get into the house." Aidan squinted at her. "We weren't a threat."

Coral tilted her head. "You gotta admit he has a point."

"I'm not saying he doesn't, but I'm telling you it was reactive." Amethyst turned her focus on me. "I think he thought you were trying to hurt the girl."

"Then why weren't they together?" That made no sense. "When she heard him, she ran."

"I'm not sure." Amethyst licked her lips. "Maybe we can find out."

"I don't know …" Aidan started.

"We need to question him anyway." I took his hand. "Might as well ask a few questions about that too."

He sighed and grinned. "Fine."

Really? I thought you would've fought me harder on this. He'd been silent the entire time we were in the bedroom. I wasn't sure if he was anxious about the wolf outside, upset with me over my decisions and actions, or a combination of the two. I was banking on the combo.

It's pointless when you do what you want anyway. He arched an eyebrow, daring me to contradict him.

I couldn't because he wasn't wrong. *Come on, let's get this over with.* "Why don't you guys come out with us? Amethyst's skills could come in handy."

"Okay."

We walked outside to find Jasper and Jabbar with Beth and Samuel. They'd chained the wolf to the tree.

"I can't believe you caught one." Jasper turned to us. "It's a good thing we had wolves staying with us."

"Were you trying to catch them?" It sounded like they'd been going out of their way to avoid them.

"At first, yes." Jabbar ran a hand through his shaggy hair. "But they evaded us, so we finally gave up. They weren't messing with anything of ours, so we were keeping a watchful eye."

"Well, you're lucky more didn't come," Aidan said and focused back on the wolf. "Now we need to wake him up."

"That we can help with," Jasper mumbled words I'd never heard before, and the wolf startled awake.

The wolf growled as his eyes landed on each person.

"Why don't you turn back into your human form so we can talk?" It was a vain request, but I had to try.

He jerked forward, but the chains snapped taut, and he fell back against the tree.

"Who's the wolf you've been following around?" Aidan closed the distance between him and the wolf, standing just far enough away so the wolf couldn't attack him.

The wolf howled and tried charging again.

"He doesn't like that question." Amethyst paced in front of him. "He doesn't want you thinking about her. He wants you to focus on him instead."

"Well, that's not very smart." I met the wolf's eyes, needing him to see that I meant what I said. "I mean, once we're done with him, we'll have all the time in the world to focus on her."

The wolf snarled and bared his teeth at me.

"She's his—" Amethyst started, but I cut her off.

"—mate." That was the only thing that made sense. But if they were mates, why weren't they together?

A tree branch snapped to the right of the house, and the black wolf charged at us. The wolf's attention was on the captive wolf until she jerked her eyes to me.

She ran straight at me, not giving a damn that everyone knew her intentions.

Her desperate need to save her mate was making her reckless.

As she jumped at me, I tapped into my wolf, allowing her to control me while in human form.

Emma, move. Aidan was only two feet away, but he was still too far to do anything given how quickly this was going down.

Just as she leapt and was in midair, aiming for my neck, I pivoted, wrapped my arm around her, and threw her to the ground. I interlocked my arms around her neck and positioned her with her legs pointing away from my body to keep her from slashing me with her claws.

She thrashed and kicked, but I increased the pressure around her neck until she began to weaken.

The chained wolf kept trying to lunge at me, but the chains held strong.

"Holy shit, she took a wolf down in human form," Beth said, her voice full of awe.

The fight soon left the white wolf, and he fell to his belly. He whimpered as he watched me, completely helpless.

After a few seconds, the girl passed out and stopped moving. Once I knew she wasn't pretending, I released my hold and stood. "Let's get them in the house. We'll force them to shift. It's time to get answers."

CHAPTER NINE

Aidan and Samuel dragged both wolves inside the house while Beth and I grabbed two kitchen chairs to restrain them in.

I hated doing this, but both were being irrational and scared, which was not a good combination.

"I'm not sure this is smart if you want them to work with you." Coral chewed on her bottom lip as she glanced at the wolves passed out on the floor.

"You do remember they attacked us less than ten minutes ago?" Aidan growled and jerked his head in her direction. Blood coated his shirt where the guy's claws had dug in. "Would you like to open us up to another attack?"

"He's right." Amethyst cupped her elbow with a hand. "We can't risk them attacking again, which they would, given the opportunity."

"Can one of you make them shift back so we can get them in the chairs?" I hated to ask since they were already struggling with the capture, but my witch magic hadn't been released.

"Yeah, I can." Amethyst lifted her hands.

After a few seconds, the two bodies began to shake. They had to be repelling the magic.

The ground underneath them shook, and something iridescent coated their fur, making it shiny.

"What the hell—" My words cut off as magic coated their bodies and their fur retracted. We hadn't seen the other guy change back at Blue Ridge. We'd come in after he was in human form, so I'd had no clue this was what the person had gone through.

Their bodies convulsed as their bones cracked, forcing them back upright. The wolves levitated as the hair disappeared.

It was awful to watch. No wonder the witches weren't keen on doing this. I closed my eyes and turned into Aidan's chest, needing him to block the image from my head.

He wrapped his arms around me, but the cracking noise was almost as bad. It wasn't like a normal shift where the body was open to it; it was literally forced. I hadn't expected it to be different.

Soon, the house stood still once more, and the girl's cry filled my ears.

"We need to lock them up now." Samuel's urgent voice broke me from my horror.

I pulled away as Aidan rushed to grab the man while Samuel handled the girl.

"Emma and Beth, get the chains," Aidan ordered. "Coral, get something to cover them."

Coral ran to the bags that were still by the door and opened hers. "I think she should fit in my clothes, and I'll grab a pair of Samuel's pants."

Shit, I needed to get my act together. I couldn't be this way. I had to be stronger.

I retrieved the chains by the door and gave one to each

guy. Beth stood between the two chairs to help the guys re-chain them.

Coral tossed some pants at Amethyst and said, "Put those on him." She then dressed the girl in pajamas.

As soon as she was dressed, Samuel picked her up and put her in the chair.

The girl's head hung, her black hair covering her face. Her skin was a paler olive like mine. As Samuel chained her hands, I went to her left side and moved her hair.

Her birthmark was similar to mine, but it only contained the lines for the right upper vertex of the star.

At least, it hadn't taken us long to find her.

"Don't touch her," a raw, raspy voice threatened.

I turned to see the guy awake and, thankfully, not naked. Luckily, Aidan had already secured his arms and was binding the bottom part of his legs because the guy grabbed for me, but the chains restrained him.

"Will you chill out?" Beth smacked the guy in the back of the head.

A snarl escaped him with hate clear in his eyes.

"I don't think that was an effective method." Coral chuckled.

"Both of you, stop." I tried to keep the smile from spreading across my face. It was so inappropriate with two people chained up after being forced back into human form. They were miserable.

Aidan got in the guy's face, showing him no fear. "Who are you?"

I wasn't sure how he'd managed that. The guy was scary as hell. His hair was almost white, but he had to be around our age—at the most, early twenties. A huge scar ran down from his right ear to his nose and was set deep in his cheek. His light blue eyes were nearly as white as his hair.

"Like I'm going to tell you shit." Spit flew from his mouth. "You're all going to pay for this."

"There are six of us against two of you." He wasn't thinking logically, so I was forced to help him think it through. "Three witches and three wolves. Do you really think you stand a chance?"

"Oh, there's one way to make him squeal." Aidan walked over to the girl and grabbed a fistful of her hair.

"Don't fucking touch her." The guy jerked toward Aidan, almost tipping the chair over.

You aren't going to hurt her. Us hurting her would not do me any favors.

Of course not, but I have to pretend like I'm willing to. Aidan's voice was calm and collected. *He's the same as the assholes back home. He won't tell you anything even if you hurt him.*

Do you think he's a member of The Hallowed Guild? If he was, why would he care about us hurting her? You'd think he'd be encouraging us to do so, but then again, mates trumped everything. That's the only reason why Aidan and I finally made it back together.

I'm not sure, but if we go by Beatrice's assumption, I'd say yes. Aidan lifted her head by the hair, causing her to stir.

"I said leave her alone." Desperation was clear in his eyes as he tried to reach Aidan once more.

"Who are you?" Aidan's tone was low.

Maybe we could play the good-cop, bad-cop angle. "Look, we don't want to hurt her or you." I lifted my hands up placatingly. Hell, I had no clue what I was doing. It was called *winging it* for a reason. "It's just ... we think she may be in danger." That wasn't a lie, and my scent would let him know that.

"You're the ones who restrained her in a chair." He

scowled, and his freaky-as-hell eyes met mine. "So ... I'm thinking you're the reason she's in danger."

"No." I tried to remain calm. "But she attacked me, so what were we supposed to do?"

"Ripping out our throats wasn't a viable option." Beth slipped through the chairs and stood next to me.

"We aren't a threat to either of you." Amethyst gave her usual kind smile that warmed her violet eyes.

"You're a fucking witch." The guy bared his teeth at her. "All of your kind wants to hurt us."

Yeah, he's The Hallowed Guild, all right. There was no denying it after that comment.

"Of course, he'd be another asshole." Coral pursed her lips and looked at Aidan. "You're almost redeemed in my eyes now."

Samuel nodded in agreement. "It does help that he's not being hateful toward us anymore."

"Are they talking about you?" The guy glared at Aidan.

"Yeah, I was raised to hate witches." Aidan tilted his head. "Let's just say our first meeting didn't go well."

The guy sneered. "But you're here with them."

Okay, I wasn't in the mood for games. "Look ..." Hell, I didn't know his name.

"Call him Sparky." Beth pointed to him. "I think it works."

"I'm not a fucking dog," he growled.

"Well, Sparky's what you got unless you want to give us your real name." Maybe we could annoy him into submission.

"Damn," the girl muttered as she tried lifting her head but couldn't due to Aidan's grip.

He dropped his hand and stepped back toward me.

She groaned and lifted her head again to survey the

room. Her eyes were still that bright blue, which seemed more pronounced with her black hair. Once they'd taken in everything, she focused back on me. "Who the fuck are you?"

"Wow, that was pleasant." It almost sounded like something Beth would say. "Maybe I'd tell you if you asked me nicer."

"You've got me chained up," she grumbled and faced the guy. "Who are you?"

"So, you two don't know each other." That confirmed our suspicions. "Then why did you two attack us to defend each other?"

"I ... I don't know." The girl sagged her head. "After these past several days, I don't understand anything."

"What do you mean?" It felt like we might actually get somewhere with her.

"You'll think I'm crazy." She rolled her head, stretching her neck.

"You might be surprised." I had to go with my gut. "I'm Emma, and I came here looking for you."

"What do you mean?" Her eyes searched for something in mine.

Let her go. I felt awful having a conversation with her still chained.

What? Aidan spun around.

We need her to trust us. How could she when we had her chained up? "If we unchain you, do you promise not to attack us again?"

She paused and then slowly nodded.

The guy stared me down. "What about me?"

"Nope, you're still a wild card." I headed to the girl's arm, but before unchaining her, I looked at Amethyst. "Is she good for it?"

"Yeah, she's curious but scared." Amethyst gave me a small nod. "But she should be good. She's not terrified like before."

"Okay." I loosened the chains so she could get her arm out.

Aidan growled but followed suit, and the girl was free within seconds.

She stood and took a few steps to get her bearings. "Okay, so I guess this has at least earned my name. I'm Gabby."

I'd take any amount of information. "And he is?"

"Like we said, we don't know each other." Her attention went to him, and her breathing increased. "He's been chasing me around since the earthquake."

There it was, the word I'd been wanting to hear. "That's when you started feeling different."

"Not really." She huffed. "I've never wanted to talk about this with anyone, so I'm not sure if I should start now."

"Don't tell them anything." The guy strained against his chains again. "They've got some kind of agenda."

"How in the hell would you know?" Beth scoffed. "Just like a man to think he knows everything."

"The only reason you're chained up is because you attacked my mate." Aidan pointed at him as his hands shook with rage.

"You were antagonizing her." The veins in his neck bulged. "She had to run off."

"I ran off because of you, not them." The girl turned on her heel to face him. "You've been stalking me for days."

"You've been alone." He licked his lips. "I couldn't let anything happen to you."

"It's creepy if you were following her without introducing yourself first," Beth's nose wrinkled with confusion.

"I wasn't thinking," he growled.

"Clearly," Coral said, her eyebrows rising.

"I don't need any input from you, shrew," he spat.

"Look, I came here for you." He was trying to rile Gabby up, trying to turn her so she didn't trust us. I needed her to stay with me. If he was her mate, he could affect her.

"Look." I turned around and moved my hair to show her my birthmark.

"Holy shit." Her words were knocked out of her. "It's like the one that popped up on me." She turned her head so I could see the one vertex.

"This could be a trick," the guy said, but his voice had lost its malice.

"No, it's not." Aidan stared at him. "They're the hybrids the original alpha warned us about."

"And the worst thing they can do is run off together." He went pale and pleaded with Gabby. "Please, listen to me. You need to stay safe."

Why isn't he freaking out about her? I'd expected some hate-filled words from him after revealing her witchy secret.

I have no clue. Aidan blinked at the guy.

Yeah, you and me both. Okay, maybe this was a good thing.

"You've been chasing me, and you attacked them." She stared at the ground as if in some sort of internal struggle. "Why would I listen to you?"

"Because, for some reason, I want to protect you even if it goes against my very being." He cringed. "And I can't risk anything happening to you."

"Do you want to go outside to talk?" Maybe she'd be more willing to open up away from everyone.

"Yeah, that's a good idea." She glanced at the witches and hurried past them like she was afraid they would hurt her.

Emma, I need to go with you. Aidan's anxiety was clear through the bond.

I need you to stay here and connect with Sparky. Someone needed to calm him. *You are the only one who can relate to him.*

If you need me, you'd better link with me instantly. He wasn't thrilled, and I couldn't blame him. There was a lot at stake, and we were taking too long to get answers. If we didn't hurry, there was no telling how hard the others would be to find.

CHAPTER TEN

Aidan

It pissed me off that she'd gone out there with the girl alone, but what could I do? Every time I tried to protect her, she got angry. Yes, she was supposed to lead, but that didn't mean my wolf and I were okay with her putting herself in harm's way.

"If she hurts her ..." the guy in the chair growled.

He was annoying me. He kept saying the same thing over and over, which gave me pause. That's probably how Emma was feeling toward me. I hated to ask this question but needed to know the truth. "Do I sound like that?"

Coral leaned back on her heels. "Overprotective?"

"Oh, hell, yeah, and you need to get a handle on it." Beth's gaze stayed on the window.

"Well, how am I supposed to be okay with that?" This would be an ongoing struggle, and Beth was right. I already had a feeling Emma would talk to me tonight after it was all said and done.

"You aren't." Amethyst shrugged. "But you have to accept it."

"You say you hated witches, and now you're pouring your heart out to them?" The dumbass scowled openly in disgust.

"Don't worry. You'll have to eat your words, too." If this was her mate, we wouldn't be leaving without him, which sucked. We didn't need another person making rounds with us. I wasn't thrilled that we had six people starting out but couldn't really fight it since we needed two vehicles.

"Yeah, right." He shook his head.

"You do realize that girl is half witch?" It's like it hadn't sunk in or something.

He squeezed his eyes shut and mumbled, "Fuck."

Yeah, I understood that sentiment all too well. "Where does your pack think you are?"

Something unreadable passed in his eyes. "They know where I am."

The stench of sulfur filled the air.

"Really? You're going to lie to a shifter?" Maybe this guy was a lot dumber than I'd thought, which was saying something.

His shoulders slumped. "They don't give a shit where I am." He moved his arms again, trying to get out of the chains. "Can I get out of this?"

Yeah, that sealed the deal. The guy was a moron. "After you attacked us, you expect me to just free you?"

"I thought you were trying to hurt her." He paused. "Now that you aren't, I won't attack."

He wasn't lying, but damn, I couldn't be sure.

"I think we should." Amethyst met my eyes. "He's telling the truth."

I linked with Emma, needing to let her know. *This guy wants to be released.*

If Amethyst thinks it's safe, it might be for the best. We need both of them willing to talk with us. Emma sounded calm and collected, which was a good thing.

That meant she wasn't feeling upset, threatened, or alarmed.

Fine, but if I tell you to take cover, please listen. Maybe he was feeling agreeable now, but that could change in an instant. "Are you going to be nice to them?" I motioned toward the witches.

"Yeah, I don't really have a choice." His creepy-ass eyes met mine. "I'm grossly outnumbered."

He had a point. I loosened the chains. "Don't make me regret this." I'd been raised not to give anyone a second chance. Hell, didn't even give them a first until they proved they deserved the opportunity. This went against everything ingrained in me. When I thought about it, not being opened to others had been my struggle ever since I'd seen that mark on Emma's neck. Now that we'd completed our bond, I knew I'd made the right decision. My dad had it wrong by teaching us not to let anyone new in, which meant he was wrong about the witches.

The guy jumped to his feet and stretched out his arms. When he looked down, he stopped. "Whose pants am I wearing?"

"Hey, I'm not too thrilled about this either." Samuel shuddered and glared at Coral. "But they're yours now."

"That's what you get for putting your shit in my bag." Coral pointed at him and narrowed her eyes.

The guy frowned. "They're tight as fuck."

Of course, this made me notice how tight they were.

The bulge was large, and there were some things you couldn't unsee. "I may have something of mine you can wear."

"What is your name, anyway?" Beth pursed her lips. "I think by what I've seen of you, I deserve a name." Her eyes were glued to his junk.

"Logan." His gaze met mine. "What's yours?"

Did he think I'd be forthcoming with him because he'd given us his name?

Amethyst took a step forward. "I'm Amethyst," she said and pointed to each of us. "That's Aidan, Beth, Coral, and Samuel." She walked to the door and let herself outside.

Okay, I guess she didn't want to be in the room with him any longer.

"Look, I didn't mean to cause any problems. When Gabby gets back, we'll head out." Logan crossed his arms over his chest.

How cute. He thought we were going to let them leave.

Emma

We were sitting on the front porch in the two wooden rocking chairs. Her eyes seemed to glow even when her wolf wasn't surging forward.

It was nice talking to Gabby. She was still hesitant, but our stories lined up and were very similar. She had no clue who her parents were, and she'd been raised by a pack that had taken mercy on her. No one set of parents had adopted her. She had kind of rotated through the pack so the burden wouldn't fall on one person. That's what broke my heart the most.

It was clear I was very fortunate that Mom and Dad had wanted me without a second thought. "Look, there are three other girls we need to find."

"I don't know ..." Gabby looked toward the house.

She didn't want to leave him. "Is he your mate?"

"I don't know." Her head snapped back around, and she focused on me. "Do you think so?"

Of course, they hadn't figured it out. "How long have you known each other?" I wondered if their story was similar to Aidan's and mine.

"I ran into him at a grocery store, and it was odd. I was drawn to him but toward this place too." She ran a hand through her hair. "It freaked me out, and I ran. He followed."

"And you were scared he might attack you?" That was the only thing that made sense.

"Yeah, I mean ... no other wolf had ever done that before." She rocked in the chair as she stared forward.

"Doesn't your pack wonder where you are?" I still couldn't get over that she was out here alone. My parents would've flipped their lid, and if not them, then Aidan.

"The alpha checks in." She flinched and lowered her voice. "He knows I'm working things out."

"So your pack is close?" I hadn't even considered that.

"Close enough. They're about twenty miles from here." She shrugged, pretending it wasn't a big deal.

"What about his pack?" We needed to make sure no one would cause an issue.

"I'm not sure. Another pack has lands about fifty miles away. Sometimes we run into each other, but we keep separate." She tapped her foot. "From what I've heard, they treat the females in the pack horribly. Don't get me wrong, our pack alpha and beta are male, but they treat us well."

"No, I get that. It's the same where I'm from." She had to have been drawn here because of the witches. "Aidan is from a pack very similar, treating their females awful. You do realize our destiny is to lead both shifters and witches."

"What?" Her mouth dropped open. "That's impossible."

Footsteps came our way, and we stood straight up.

Olive came into view and focused on Gabby. "The twins told me you caught the wolves that were stalking us."

"I ..." Gabby's eyes widened, and her mouth opened and closed.

"She's the one we came here looking for." I touched Gabby's arm to calm her down.

"Who are you?" Olive came onto the porch with us and glared at the girl.

The girl was paralyzed with fear.

"She's like me." I pointed to my left ear. "She has a partial of my birthmark."

"Let me see." Olive motioned for the girl to move her hair.

Gabby complied, which surprised me.

"Well, I guess you're welcome here, then." Olive held her hand out. "I'm Olive, the head priestess of the coven."

"I heard witches can't be trusted." Gabby's voice was full of concern but not malice.

"That partial pentagram proves you're part witch." Olive lifted her chin. "So are you going to insult me further by refusing my hand?"

Wow, okay. The woman had some attitude. "It's fine." We didn't need to insult her. There's no telling if we'd need their help in the future.

"Sorry." She reached out, and when their hands touched, Gabby jerked back like she'd been shocked.

"Dear God, you're tied to this coven." Olive stepped back, breathing fast.

"Is that why I've been feeling drawn here?" Gabby asked, her voice filled with hope. "How do you know, though?"

Amethyst joined us and closed the door behind her. She stepped forward to explain since Olive had gone still. "Each time we touch another witch, there is a hum. It's slightly different for each coven so we can recognize one of our own."

Damn. Her timing was always impeccable.

"Yes, but that means ..." Olive's eyes watered, and a sob wracked her body. "That means Anna isn't coming home."

"Anna?" She would have to be a little more specific.

"My daughter." Olive dabbed her eyes as a tear rolled down her cheek. "She was seeing a wolf shifter, and I warned her, but she didn't listen. She ran off with him ..." She gasped for breath as snot ran from her nose. "I thought she'd come back, but she didn't. That means ..."

She didn't need to say more. We both knew how that story ended.

"What does it mean?" Gabby stood and glanced between Olive and me.

"She died." I hated to say the words after seeing how much yearning was in Gabby's eyes. "Witches die when they give birth to half shifters."

Her forehead lined with confusion. "But I thought witches and wolves couldn't reproduce."

"They can when it's time for us to be born." It sounded surreal, but it was true.

"So, you're my grandmother?" Her eyes flicked to Olive's.

"Yes, child." She pulled the girl into her arms. "I

should've known with those haunting blue eyes you have. They are just like hers."

It felt rude to be out there with them. "I'll go in. Gabby, will you come in when you're done?"

"Yeah." She nodded, but her eyes didn't move from mine.

I walked back into the house, pulling Amethyst with me, and found the five others standing around awkwardly.

The guy's eyes landed right on me. "Where's Gabby?"

"She's out there with Olive." I wasn't sure why I needed to explain myself to him, but for some damn reason, I did.

"Hell, no," he growled and marched to the door.

"This isn't good." Amethyst's eyes met mine. "Logan, calm down."

I crossed my arms, blocking the way out.

"Move out of the way, or I'll make you." His voice was low and angry.

"Hey, asshole," Aidan rasped. "You don't talk to my mate that way."

"She's out there with her grandmother." I stared down my nose at Logan. "So give them a minute."

"Her grandmother?" Beth turned toward me and scratched her head. "Things are getting so strange."

I understood that sentiment. "I promise she's not in any danger," I said, hoping to appease his wolf a little bit.

"Fine. She has five minutes." He paced between the couch and the kitchen.

A huge yawn left me, and I realized how tired I was. We'd been going for over fourteen hours, and we'd just been in a huge fight. My adrenaline was crashing.

The front door opened, nearly bumping me in the back. I was shocked that the two of them were coming in so soon.

I spun around and saw the devastated state Olive was in. Her skin, which had seemed youthful, was now pale and unhealthy. Finding out your daughter was dead had to be a hard fact to take in.

Olive sniffed and met my eyes. "I'll get the twins to bring some air mattresses for those two," she said as her eyes focused on the shirtless wolf shifter, "to sleep on. We can meet for breakfast as we discussed."

"Okay, thank you." I forced a smile, but even I could feel it was lacking.

"Let's get everything situated so we can get you into bed." Aidan grabbed our two bags from the entryway.

"I'll put up a perimeter spell." Samuel followed his lead and placed the small bag on top of a duffle bag.

"Who said I was staying here?" Logan took Gabby's arm. "We're going."

"No, I'm staying here." She removed her arm from his grip. "If you want to go, go."

His brows furrowed. "I'm not leaving without you."

"Then, I guess you're staying." Beth snorted as she picked up her luggage. "Come on, Gabby. We can room together. That way, Samuel and Logan can stay out here together."

"Okay," Gabby agreed quickly and stepped away from Logan.

Even though I didn't know her well, I knew what she was feeling. I had two parents who loved me, and I was afraid of rejection, so her fears had to be worse. She probably didn't let anyone close, and her feelings for Logan probably scared her.

"Like I said, I'll set the perimeter spell so these two can't escape without us knowing." Samuel waved us on. "The rest of you can go to bed. We all need rest. It sounds like we'll be leaving here tomorrow."

He was right. After breakfast, we'd need to cut out and head to the next spot.

"Are you sure you don't need any help?" Coral offered.

"Nope, go on."

That's all it took.

WHEN AIDAN and I entered the bedroom and shut the door, I turned on my heel to face him. I opened my mouth, but he held his hand up, stopping me.

"Look, I know what you're going to say." He put our bags down, walked over to me, and placed his hands on my waist. "I'm sorry about the way I acted tonight. I know you're strong, and these are the things that need to be done, but dammit ... do you know how hard this is for me, too?"

Well, alrighty then. I hadn't expected this. "I know." I placed my hand against his cheek, enjoying the feel of his stubble against my skin. "And I'm sorry. I don't like seeing you in these situations either."

"Can't we just run away?" A small smile played at the corners of his lips, but I knew better. If I said yes, he'd whisk me away in a heartbeat, and it made me love him more.

"When this is all over ..." I stood on my tiptoes and kissed him. "... we'll have to be partners in this. I can't do this without you, but there are certain risks I must take."

"Why do you have to be so reasonable?" he murmured as he kissed me once more.

My body warmed, but I was just too tired.

"Come on, let's get you some rest. Tomorrow is a big

day." He turned off the lights and tugged me toward the queen-sized bed in the center.

I hadn't even scanned the room before I crawled into bed. He scooted in beside me. When he wrapped his arms around me, I drifted off despite the uneasy feeling that pulsed through my skin.

CHAPTER ELEVEN

Aidan

A loud thud woke me from my sleep, which angered me. I wasn't ready to get up, not with Emma still sleeping so soundly in my arms.

"Dude, watch it." My ears perked up at Samuel's low voice.

That asshole was going to make me get up.

I slowly unwrapped myself from my mate's body, which was damn hard to do. If this hadn't meant so much to her, I'd have ignored it and not given a damn. But if Logan got free and alerted the other Hallowed Guild members or hurt Samuel, I couldn't live with myself.

The room had beige carpeting. Thankfully, it would soften my footsteps as I snuck out. Emma needed to rest. Considering how often shit went down, we'd probably be in another crisis before the day was over. It sounded like it might already have started.

I somehow managed to not wake her as I detangled myself from her. She was out cold.

I grabbed the black shirt off the floor and put it back on. Then, I stood and picked up my jeans. The last thing I needed was to go out there with my junk on display.

It was clear this room wasn't used often. It was bare except for the bed and the bathroom off to the left.

"You're going to wake everyone up," Samuel said with annoyance.

"So what?" Logan asked as he stomped through the house. "Gabby and I need to get out of here."

Of course, he'd be planning on leaving with her. However, that wasn't an option. I turned the knob slowly and opened the door, waiting for a creak. Thank goodness, it didn't happen. I hurried into the hallway and shut the door.

I tiptoed into the living room and frowned. "Will you two keep it down?" I whispered.

Logan rolled his eyes. "I'm just picking up my stuff." He stood on top of his air mattress, pushing all the air out. "We need to get out of here before those witches come back."

"You do realize those witches are Gabby's family?" He had to understand that this wouldn't disappear. I'd foolishly wished that Emma's mark would disappear when I was younger, but seeing her at the University, being hunted down, made me realize I couldn't ignore it any longer. I still let my hate guide me, and it took almost losing Emma for me to finally realize that she was so much more important than anything else—even my hate.

"They could be lying." Logan sucked in a breath. "Witches are known to do that."

"Then how can you justify her birthmark behind her ear?" He needed to see logic and fast. The longer it took, the longer it would take us to leave. They were mates; there was no doubt about that.

"You guys could have Sharpied it on her." He got off the mattress and scowled. "They've got you hook, line, and sinker."

Aidan? Emma's voice rang in my head. *Where are you?*

The bastard had woken her up. *I'm in here with Logan and Samuel.*

Is everything all right? she asked, and I heard the bed creak from her getting up.

It will be. I didn't want to worry her more than she already was, but she'd be here within seconds. "Do you actually believe that?" He was paranoid, which made him dangerous.

"Who the hell knows?" he said louder.

A door down the hallway opened, and two sets of footsteps headed our way.

Great, he'd woken everyone up.

Beth's and Gabby's flowery scents hit me before they entered the room.

"You're leaving?" Gabby's forehead crinkled, and hurt flashed in her eyes.

"No, we're leaving," Logan grumbled as he folded the mattress up.

"I don't believe I made that decision." Gabby's tone was tight and laced with anger.

Oh, I remembered that tone all too well. It was the very one Emma had used on me back at Crawford.

Emma

I HEARD the conversation clear as day as I quickly threw on my pink shirt and jeans and headed to the door. Logan was determined to leave with Gabby, and unfortunately, I couldn't let that happen. If I couldn't convince her to help us find the next girl, we all might end up dead or worse.

With a sigh, I flung the door open and stalked into the living room where everyone else was.

"Dammit!" Coral yelled from the bedroom she and Amethyst were sharing. "And you complained we were loud that one day when you stayed over."

Under normal circumstances, I'd have laughed, but right now, I had a feeling another war was brewing.

What the hell is she talking about? Aidan looked at me.

After Jacob got hurt at the game, we stayed with them. He knew that. He'd been standing outside of my dorm, watching the whole thing. *Coral came down that next morning, and she thought she was being quiet, but she woke the three of us up.*

Three of you? Aidan's voice was tense, but that was it.

He thought Jacob and I had shared a bed. *Yes, they had two love seats and a couch in the living room. We each took one.*

"Look, I'm not going." Gabby laughed without humor. "But feel free to go."

"I'm not leaving without you." He glared at her as his freaky eyes glowed. "Get your stuff, and let's get out of here."

"You don't get to tell me what to do." Gabby closed the distance and pushed her finger in his chest. "You aren't and never will be my alpha."

At least, she wasn't ready to hightail it out of here. "Look, she's marked, and we need her to break the prophecy or curse ... whatever you consider it. If she doesn't leave with me to help find the other girls, we're all at risk."

"You being together would be even riskier." Logan's

eyes flicked to me, and he frowned. "It'd be stupid. The Hallowed Guild could take you out in one fell swoop."

Gabby asked with confusion. "Hallowed Guild?"

"It's the secret society that wants us dead." That was a blunt description, but it worked.

"What? Why?" She wrapped her arms around her body and hugged herself. "How am I nineteen and don't know any of this?"

I was surprised that she was older than me.

Aidan filled her in on all the details. We'd probably have to inform the other girls as well. At least, she and I hadn't known anything about the curse or the secret society.

"Oh my God." Gabby's eyes landed on me. "That's awful."

"It is, and if we find the others, we can finally end the war between shifters and witches." She needed to understand how important this was.

"But I don't want to leave." She took a step back. "This could be a whole misunderstanding."

I hadn't been prepared for her to not want to go. I'd assumed once she'd heard the story she'd be in. "You have to."

A low growl came from Logan's throat, but Gabby ignored him.

A fist pounded on the door, interrupting the tension in the room.

It's Olive. Aidan opened the door.

"I see you're all up." Olive gazed around the room and settled on her granddaughter. "Is something wrong?"

"She wants me to leave here." Gabby glanced at the ground as she shook her head. "But I don't want to."

"Oh, honey. I don't want you to either." Olive walked across the room, her earth-brown gown flowing behind her.

She pulled her granddaughter into her chest. "Especially since I just found you, but this is too important to turn your back on."

"But what if the prophecy is wrong?" Gabby stepped out of the hug and grabbed Olive's hand. "What if leaving is the wrong decision?"

"You have to leave with us. It's not negotiable." I wanted to cringe at the words; they sounded a lot like Logan's, but this was for the good of our race.

"Once again, you aren't my alpha." Her body stiffened as she turned to me. "Just because you're the golden one doesn't mean shit to me."

"I told you we needed to leave." Logan stepped toward her as if he intended to grab her and take off.

Aidan stood in front of the door and crossed his arms. He was ready to fight to make sure Gabby didn't leave with anyone but us.

"If you think she's not going with us, we have a problem." Aidan squared his shoulders, making it known he didn't plan on backing down.

"It may not mean shit to you, but you're leaving with us." I couldn't waver. Maybe this was the first real test of my destiny.

"I'm tired of the two of you telling me what to do." A cruel smirk appeared on her face. "There's only one way I'll leave the family I just found."

I had a feeling I knew where this was going. It was the way of the wolves. She'd found something she wasn't willing to give up unless she found me worthy.

"We fight. If you win, I go with you. If I win, I stay with my grandmother." Gabby stared me down, letting her strength shine through. "Only the two of us. I'm not petrified anymore. I had all night to think, and staying here is important to me. So convince me leaving is actually worthwhile."

Aidan linked with me. *Absolutely not.*

But he didn't get to make that call. I did. "Deal."

"No, unacceptable." Logan's body stiffened.

"I hate to tell you two macho dudes, but the ladies just agreed." Beth pointed at me and winked. "And my girl has this."

Yeah, I hoped I did.

"Then, there's no time like the present." Gabby headed to the door and stopped in front of Aidan. "So move."

"Maybe this isn't wise," Olive said.

"I would usually agree with her, but Emma has this." Aidan looked at me with pride. *You beat her ass last night.*

Yeah, let's hope it ends the same way. I tried to sound confident for him.

"Can they even back down now?" Samuel looked at me and then at Gabby. "Isn't that like some kind of animal code?"

He was right. Neither of our wolves were willing to back down. "Let's do this so we can head out for the next girl." I had to sound confident even if I wasn't.

"Coral! Amethyst!" Beth yelled over her shoulder. "You don't want to miss this."

Not bothering to deal with Beth's antics, I approached Aidan and pressed my lips to his. *I'll be fine.*

Damn straight you will be. He wrapped his arms around my waist and pulled me closer.

I had a feeling he was alluding to knowing I'd win. He wouldn't hesitate to step in, which meant I couldn't lose.

"Let's go." Gabby walked around Aidan and opened the door.

I pulled away from him and grinned. I turned and followed her to where we'd fought last night.

The others followed behind.

"It's not to the death." I wanted to make that clear. Neither one of us needed to be taken out. If we were to fight to the death, we'd be handing The Hallowed Guild a victory without them doing a damn thing. "And in human form." I didn't want to ruin the few pairs of clothes I had left.

"Fine." Gabby stood in front of me and raised her fists.

You need to take her hard and fast. Aidan linked with me, and he was so tense even the words spoken through our bond were clenched. *No one ever expects it. She'll go for your neck like last night. Her wolf will control it.*

Okay, it wouldn't hurt to try.

I glanced behind me and realized that only the wolves were out here. Samuel, Olive, Amethyst, and Coral were in the house, watching through the window.

Logan stood next to Aidan with his arms crossed. They were like carbon copies with the unpleasantness radiating off their bodies.

"I'll be the referee since those two idiots will try to stop the fight at the first punch." Beth motioned to us. "So, go."

I crouched into a fighting position, and Gabby stood straight as if she didn't have a care in the world. Aidan wanted me to attack first, but my gut said no.

Just as I'd expected, she took off toward me, rearing her arm back to punch me in the face.

I could end this now, but it would be a huge blow to her ego. I ducked, causing her hand to catch air. Straightening, I kicked her hard right in the stomach.

"Ugh," she groaned, stumbling back several feet.

"I thought you wanted to fight," I goaded her.

You need to end this, Aidan said with concern. *You don't need to get hurt.*

Don't worry. I got back into a fighter's stance. *I'm only humoring her.*

Displeasure pulsed through our bond, but he didn't say another word.

She ran at me again, her focus right on my stomach. I wasn't sure what she planned, but at least I knew her target.

I forced myself to wait until the last second before spinning to the side. She hadn't expected the move and stumbled forward, landing on her knees.

She pounded the ground. "I'm just getting started." She jumped to her feet, her knees dirty, and swung at me.

I blocked her punch and countered with my own. My fist connected with her chest, knocking the wind out of her.

Her breathing became ragged, and Logan growled beside me.

He's about to lose his shit. Aidan moved closer to me. *End it now.*

She bent over and took a few gasping breaths. "Now, I'm pissed." She ran at me again, letting her emotions rule her.

At the last second, I bent over, causing her to only hit air, and her body stumbled over mine. I used her momentum against her and straightened my back. She fell to the side. Right before she hit the ground, I spun around and put her in a headlock.

This was what I'd done to her last night while she'd been in wolf form. Aidan was right—it was her weakness. She didn't focus on anything but the kill.

She bucked underneath me, and I heard Aidan growl, "Stay out of it. She's not hurting her."

"Like hell, she's not," Logan grunted.

I heard the crunching of bone.

Gabby stopped fighting.

Both of us locked in on the huge man on the ground. Aidan stood over him. Blood poured from Logan's nose, but he got back to his feet.

"Fine, I give up." Gabby sighed, forcing the words out. "I'll go with you. Just leave him alone."

"Gladly." Aidan retreated a few steps but kept his eyes on Logan in case he attacked.

"This was a little anticlimactic." Beth pouted but then shrugged. "But you gave up, so it's an official loss. No fighting dirty."

"I said I give up," Gabby growled.

"Okay." I released my hold on her and stood. "We need to leave immediately."

"If she goes, so do I." Logan wiped the blood from his nose with his hand.

"We figured you'd be coming along," Aidan grumbled. "But what are you going to tell your pack?"

Logan's jaw clenched. "They don't care where I am."

"Why the hell not?" Aidan tensed and jerked his head in his direction. *He's too risky to bring along.*

Doesn't matter. He'll follow us. Dammit, each time we made progress, something held us back.

"My sister mated with the alpha." Logan stared off into the trees. "And one night, I saw him beating on her. I attacked him."

Oh shit. I knew what his next words would be.

"They rejected me for going against the alpha." He rubbed a hand down his face. "Banishment was my punishment."

The air was clear of any lie.

Aidan tensed. "So you're a rogue?"

Their stories were very similar, but Aidan had our bond to rely on. He wasn't truly alone.

"Yes, but so far, I've been okay." He focused on Gabby. "Because of her."

Gabby sucked in a breath. "Then I guess you better come with us."

At least, that was one thing we didn't have to worry about. "What about your pack?" If no one had truly taken her in, it made me nervous that I'd told them the truth.

"I'll tell them I've met up with some wolves and am going with you all." Gabby winced as if it hurt to admit. "They won't care."

"Fine, but you leave your cell phones here." Aidan glanced from one to the other. "We have to make sure no one tracks us."

"I don't have a cell phone. I lost it a while ago when I shifted and went hunting for Gabby." Logan nodded.

It was all settled. "Well, let's go get Amethyst to help us with the locator spell." I motioned for Gabby to follow me, and thankfully, she complied.

When we walked back inside the house, Olive rushed over to her. "It's for the best. You need to help them."

Gabby's shoulders drooped. "It's just that I want to get to know you."

"When this is all over, you're welcome to go wherever you want." I would never force someone to stay with me. "We just need to break this curse first."

"Can you have breakfast with us before you leave?" Hope filled Olive's eyes as they met mine.

"Sure. Let us pack up, and we'll head over." I'd hate not to let them have a little more time together. They'd gone so long without knowing each other.

"Great. My house is the one right across." She pointed

across the road and inhaled. "Just come on in. I'll cook enough for all." She hurried out of the house.

I turned to Amethyst. "Do you have the map to do the locator spell?" The sooner we knew where we were going, the better.

"Yeah, it's in the bedroom." Amethyst ran down the hall.

Gabby's eyes went to Samuel and Coral. "What do we have to do for that spell?"

Trying to encourage her, Samuel grinned. "Just a little bit of your blood."

"Oh, hell no." Logan shook his head. "Blood is the most powerful thing a witch can have."

"Trust me when I say they're just going to ignore you." Aidan huffed and leaned back on his heels. "Believe me."

"Why do we need to use our blood?" Gabby chewed on her lip. "In TV shows, they always need something of the person you're looking for."

Amethyst came back into the room. "That's true, but you all are interconnected with the original witch's magic," she explained as she laid the map on the table. "Using Emma's blood was how we found you. From what the original witch's journal says, the combination of blood from the two of you will find the third girl, and so on."

Needing to make Gabby feel more at ease, I bit into my fingertip and dribbled my blood in the center of the map. Just like last time, my blood crept to the very spot we were now standing in.

"Holy shit, that's scary." Gabby took in a deep breath and then bit into her finger too. She placed her hand over where my blood had settled and let the blood drip onto the same spot.

Amethyst mumbled some words I couldn't understand, and then our blood began to inch northwest.

"That's impossible," Logan gasped as he watched the map with us.

The blood settled in the south-east side of North Dakota, right on Jamestown.

"We head here," I said, stating the obvious. "That has to be at least a full day's trip."

Coral tapped on her phone and said on an exhale. "It's a nineteen-hour drive."

Great, we'd thought the almost twelve-hour drive had been bad. Nineteen might kill us if The Hallowed Guild didn't find us first.

CHAPTER TWELVE

It was a rough two days of traveling to Jamestown. Ten hours in a car was not natural for either wolves or witches. Our nerves were frayed, and piling into two hotel rooms wasn't ideal. However, we were trying to keep our expenses down since Aidan, Beth, and I couldn't use our cards in case someone was tracking us. We also wanted to keep our scents to a minimum in case anyone from the Guild was in the area.

Beatrice had called the local coven, but they had turned down our request to stay there, which was odd. No one was certain why, but witches rarely declined such a simple request.

We pulled into the Hampton Inn in the town and parked to the side.

Aidan linked with me as he looked at me. *We're getting our own damn room tonight. I can't deal with Logan's and Beth's snoring another night.*

It had been god-awful. They'd kept me, Aidan, and even Gabby up all night, which had led to even shorter fuses. *You know what, let's spring for it. I have some cash.*

No, we need to keep that in case of an emergency. Aidan opened the driver's door. *I have some money saved in a checking account only in my name. We can use that.*

I wanted to argue, but this wasn't a battle worth fighting over. He had a right to be part of the decisions and make a few of his own. I loved him because he was strong, and that was something I never wanted to change.

"Do you think I can get some earplugs here?" Gabby muttered as she climbed out of the car behind Logan.

"I do not snore," Beth whined as she slammed the car door behind her.

"That doesn't prove anything." I shut the door. "It's more like denial."

"You never said anything back in the dorm." Beth strutted to the back of the car, snagged her bag, and threw it over her shoulder. "So, I don't believe you."

"That's because you didn't then." She'd snored a little, but nothing like last night.

"Maybe it's the change of altitude," Coral said as she, Samuel, and Amethyst joined us.

"What?" Beth's face scrunched. "That's not a thing."'

"Actually, it is." Samuel chuckled. "It's a medical condition."

"It's nothing to be ashamed of." Amethyst patted Beth on the shoulder. "You can't help it."

"If it's any consolation, you were quieter than Logan." I glanced over to the odd man. "He sounded like a chainsaw."

"I'm a man." Logan's face was unreadable, but his tone implied he could be joking.

"Wait ... are you trying to be funny?" Beth startled, and her face wrinkled.

Logan pursed his lips. "I can be personable."

"You might want to try smiling more, then." Gabby

smacked his shoulder. "You're kind of grouchy and broody. Maybe a smile or a chuckle every now and then would make you more approachable."

Coral tapped her chin. "She has a point."

"Let's head inside." Aidan yawned. "I need to get some sleep."

I pulled my phone from my pocket and saw it was close to nine at night. It had been a long day, especially since I'd checked on Dad again. They'd convinced Jacob to come back home with them and left without incident. Apparently, Prescott and Bradley were consumed with finding us, but my pack was worried that the Murphy's and Jones's packs might try to attack them. Just another thing to worry about. I had to fix all of this before things got worse.

Aidan was right: we needed our rest. "That way we can get up early and start looking for the girl."

"Are we just going to drive around, looking for a birthmark behind a girl's ear?" Gabby walked toward the entrance of the hotel room.

"Maybe." I wasn't sure yet.

"What?" She paused and turned around to look at me. "I was being sarcastic."

"Well, to be fair, we don't have a solid plan yet." She expected me to have answers, but dammit, I was new to all this shit, too.

"We found you, didn't we?" Aidan sounded annoyed.

"Because you were with the witches." The hate in Logan's response rang clear.

They both didn't like the way their mates were being spoken to, which was sweet, but it would only cause more problems.

"She asked a fair question, and Aidan was right about us finding her." This whole hostility thing was getting to be too much, and I hoped it would end soon. "We need to act like our own pack, even if it's not official, and talk things out." I paused, forcing myself to stay calm. "That night, I was tugged toward you, so maybe that will happen again."

"Maybe." She shrugged, but I could tell she wanted to argue.

As we walked into the hotel, our group quieted.

Aidan and Amethyst took the lead and headed to the dark wood counter to get our rooms in order while our group stood in the wide-open lobby, right in front of the open bar.

"Fate has a way of making things work out," Coral said as she smiled at us. "Who would've thought this group would be standing here, in the middle of nowhere? We got this far. She won't let us down now."

"Now that I can agree with." Gabby's eyes warmed as if the words had struck a chord with her. "But why did fate make me an orphan with no one to truly love me?" Her mouth dropped open, and she covered it with a hand.

She hadn't meant to say that last part.

"You're loved," Logan replied, his voice raspy as he looked at her.

"Am I?" she said breathlessly and stepped toward him.

I remembered those feelings all too well. Who was I kidding? I still felt like that with Aidan.

"It was bad enough to watch you and Aidan be grossly lovesick. Now I have to watch them too?" Beth grumbled and pouted.

"All right, we got our rooms." Amethyst held up two keys.

"Same room assignments as last night?" Beth asked.

"Nope. Emma and I have our own room." Aidan grinned while holding up his own key.

"Nope, not happening." Beth jerked her head from side to side and crossed her arms. "I am not rooming with those two alone. I'm staying with you." She pointed at the witches.

"There are only two beds." Samuel frowned at her. "There isn't a rollout."

"Then, I guess I'm sleeping with you." Beth glared as if daring him to disagree.

His mouth dropped open. "What?"

"Don't worry. I don't bite." She grabbed his arm, keeping him with her. "You aren't my type, so you're safe."

Of course, she'd go there. "As fun as this is, I'm heading to our room." I looped my arm through Aidan's. "Let's meet downstairs for breakfast at eight."

"Okay, see you." Beth waved.

"Wait ... you can't sleep with us if you're snoring that loudly." Coral's tone was absolute.

"Well, then one of you is staying with me," Beth growled. "I won't be alone in there when they start doing the horizontal tango."

"Really?" Samuel asked. "Horizontal tango?"

Aidan linked with me as we stepped into the elevator. *Aren't you so glad we got away from them tonight?*

Uh, yeah. My body was already warming at the thought of us being alone.

We got off the elevator on the third floor and were in our room within seconds.

As soon as the door shut, Aidan dropped our bag to the ground and pulled me into his chest. His lips were on me in a flash. *It's been too damn long.* His words were almost a sigh in my head. His fingers slipped under my shirt and dug into my skin.

It turned me on so much. I didn't care if I had bruises in the morning.

My brain fogged as I kissed him back fervently. I needed him so much. I grabbed the bottom of his shirt and lifted it, parting from his lips.

He pulled it over his head and tossed it aside.

My hands greedily rubbed all down his chest, enjoying the warm buzzing between our skin and the feel of his abs. *You're so sexy.*

And you're fucking gorgeous. He clutched my shirt and removed it, letting our chests touch. In the next second, he unfastened my bra, and I flung it to this hotel chain's standard tan colored carpet.

He lifted me, and I wrapped my legs around his waist. His kisses were desperate and hungry, which torched my body.

As he lowered me to the bed, on top of the white comforter, I bit his lip.

You're killing me, he growled.

Good. The feel of his body on mine intoxicated me. I lowered my hand to the waistband of his jeans and tugged. *Off.*

Maybe I'm not in the mood to listen. He captured my arms and held them still on either side of my head. He kissed down my neck to my breasts. He then greedily took my nipple into his mouth and flicked his tongue. Pleasure coursed through my body.

I panted as I stared at the white ceiling. *Oh, God.*

He lowered his body on top of mine and rubbed his hardness against my core. I bucked against him, needing more.

After a second, I yanked my wrists from his grip and pushed him over so I could climb on top. I raised my hips so

I could unbutton his jeans and then stood to yank them off. As soon as he was naked, my eyes devoured him, and I removed any barrier that could come between us.

He scooted against the dark wood headboard, waiting for me.

And I didn't hesitate to respond. I straddled him and guided him inside me, lowering ever so slowly onto him.

A guttural groan filled him. *Faster, please.*

You punished me for a second, so now it's my turn. I moved up and down slowly, letting the friction build. He leaned forward and captured my breast in his mouth.

We moved in unison, taking our time and enjoying the privacy and solitude we finally had.

Every time we connected, our bond strengthened.

All too soon, an orgasm rocked through our bodies. With our connection, we shared each other's pleasure on top of our own, making the experience mind-blowing.

As soon as our bodies were done, I rolled over, and he wrapped his arms around my waist. Within seconds, I was out cold.

The hotel's breakfast options were pitiful, but the meal was included with our stay, so I would make it count.

The eight of us sat at one table, and Samuel was the one with dark circles under his eyes today. He sat at the end of the table, right in front of Aidan. Beth sat next to him, directly in front of me. Gabby was between Beth and Logan while Amethyst sat next to me with Coral on the other end on our side.

"You weren't kidding when you said those two snore." He took a bite of waffle and frowned. "It was like a never-ending freight train. I kept waiting on the caboose, but it never came."

"You're the caboose," Beth snapped.

"What? That doesn't even make sense." Samuel sighed as he chewed. "If we do this again, I'm running to a store. I'll need some earplugs pronto."

"You should get us all a pair." I was sure we'd wind up rooming with Beth and Logan again before it was all over.

Gabby yawned as she laid her head on Logan's shoulder. His eyes darkened to a near blue color at her touch.

"We need to finish up and get on the road." Aidan squeezed my leg lovingly. "Do you feel a tug right now?"

"No." I'd hoped that something would lead us to her, but nothing tugged at me. "Maybe we need to drive around and see if either Gabby or I feel anything."

"I'm so glad you two have such an amazing plan." Logan dropped his fork on his plate and closed his eyes. "It's good to know that you've dragged Gabby out here when you don't have a fucking clue what to do."

Aidan tensed beside me, ready to come to my defense.

Let me try. I took his hand and rubbed my finger along his thumb. "Well, by all means, tell us what we should do."

Logan blanched, and his shoulders tensed. "Well ..."

"Oh, you're speechless?" Beth tilted her head and opened her mouth in fake shock. "I figured with how you run your mouth, you'd have answers."

"Well, you know how those alpha males are." Coral batted her eyes at Logan. "Quick to criticize but unable to provide any solutions."

"Hey now," he growled too loudly with humans around.

"No, you deserve that." Gabby sat straight and smacked him in the arm. "All you've been is an ass to them."

"Says the girl who didn't want to come and tried to get

out of it by fighting Emma." Logan didn't miss a beat in calling her out.

"It was because I'd found my family and was afraid to leave," she murmured. "But I'm glad she won. She was right; I need to be part of this. This is what I'm meant to do. I feel it now." Her eyes widened. "I really feel it. Do you?"

A slight tug pulled at me that I hadn't noticed before. "Yeah, I do." I grabbed the last piece of bacon on my plate and stuffed it in my mouth. "We need to go."

"Okay." Amethyst nodded and grabbed her plate. "Let's go find our girl."

We'd been driving around the heart of Jamestown for thirty minutes. It was a small town, so it was a good thing we weren't here to sightsee.

We took a main road away from the city and into the less populated outskirts, which didn't surprise me. I had a feeling she wasn't in the city center. It would have been too easy to find her there.

Everyone was tense and uneasy in the vehicle. The witches followed behind us since Gabby and I were the two who would lead us to her.

After another thirty minutes, the tugging became stronger. "Turn right here." I pointed to a gravel road that led into dense trees.

"Okay." Aidan slowed down, and just as we completed the turn, Samuel honked the horn twice behind us.

"What the hell?" Beth complained in the very back of the suburban. "They can't call us, for God's sake?"

Aidan stopped the car, and Amethyst jumped out of the

passenger seat and ran to my window. This was kind of strange.

I rolled it down. "What's up?"

"We need to go the rest of the way on foot." Amethyst stared down the road.

"Why?" We couldn't just leave our cars here.

"Because you're leading us to the coven that doesn't want us to visit." Amethyst frowned. "So we need to be careful and stake it out before forcing our way in."

It caught me off guard even though it shouldn't have. The witches were hiding her, so we had to be careful not to start another war.

CHAPTER THIRTEEN

We parked the vehicles several miles away from the road that led to the coven. We'd found a gravel pull-off area. Trees surrounded the area, so we'd parked in the corner section, praying the trees would hide us enough so no one would stop to check on the vehicles. If we wanted to stay undetected, we had to at least try to be inconspicuous.

As we all clambered out of the vehicle, I asked the group of witches, "How did you know we were heading toward the coven?"

"Mom told me where it is," Amethyst said as she shut her door and approached me. Her blonde hair was tied in a ponytail, and her purple eyes seemed vibrant. "She visited here several years ago, and in case something happened, she gave me the address." Her black sweater bunched at the shoulders as she pointed into the woods.

"Why are we surprised that witches are involved?" Logan grumbled as he held out his hand to help Gabby out of the car.

"I'm not handicapped, you know?" Gabby pushed his

hand away and got out of the car. She pulled her light tan sweatshirt over her jeans and glared at him.

"I was being gentlemanly," Logan growled, hurt reflected in his eyes.

He was trying to be a mate to her, but she wasn't ready, and her wolf wanted to be strong. Maybe she was to be trying to prove something to us ... or hell, maybe just to herself.

You might need to talk to him. They aren't on the same page. In a way, their situation was quite the opposite of Aidan's and mine.

Yeah, but you'll need to talk to her too. Aidan stepped around the car and took my hand.

You're right. It wasn't just her working through stuff; he was too. He'd lost his pack and family from the sounds of it.

"What about me?" Beth climbed out of the car and placed her hands on her hips, glaring right at Logan. "You weren't gentlemanly to me."

"With a mouth like yours, I figured you didn't need anyone's help." He lowered his chin to look down on her.

"Oh, dear God." Samuel marched between them. "I don't have the patience to deal with you two after what I had to attempt to sleep through last night."

"And you aren't even a wolf shifter." Aidan closed his eyes. "So imagine how much worse it was for Emma and me."

"Are we going to stand around and shoot the shit all day, or are we going to get moving?" Standing on the outskirts of our circle, Coral lifted both hands.

She was right. It was time to get moving. There was no telling what we'd have to deal with or how long it would take. "Let's go."

"Remember, we have to move slower." Aidan nodded

toward the witches. "They need to be able to keep up and not make any noise."

"Got it." Gabby took a few steps toward the woods.

"Wait ... what if they have a perimeter spell?" If they were guarding something, it made sense that they would be protecting their space.

"Does it really matter?" Coral crossed her arms. "If there is a perimeter spell, are we gonna quit and head back home?"

"We'll have to cross that bridge when we get there," Aidan answered. "We won't know how to react until we see how they take us being here."

That was a good point. If they were angry, we'd have to deal with that differently than if they were annoyed. There were so many different scenarios, and we couldn't plan them all ahead of time.

"Fine, but follow my lead." Amethyst glanced at the wolves. "Got it?"

"Of course." She was a witch and the next priestess of her coven, so they'd listen to her the most.

"No time like the present." I let go of Aidan's hand and led the group into the woods.

Our group moved slowly but steadily. The deeper we got into the woods, the more I expected to see animals running around or hear birds chirping, but it was silent. *Don't you find it odd that there are no animals around?*

I led the pack, letting the pull take me to where the girl was, with Aidan right behind me.

His footsteps were silent as he linked back with me. *Yeah, we need to be careful. Animals don't run away from witches like this.*

Unfortunately, they usually only ran away from predators, which would probably mean wolves. *Do you think it might be The Hallowed Guild?*

Maybe. Aidan paused. *Most likely, but I don't smell them.*

That didn't mean anything. I held up my hand, telling the others to stop. *We need to alert them to the possibility.*

Fine, but we have to be very quiet. Aidan turned around, and the eight of us huddled.

"There might be shifters nearby." Maybe it was coincidental, but with our luck, it wasn't.

"So what do we do?" Coral looked around as if she expected a wolf to attack us.

"You three stay here." It was smarter to limit the number of those scoping the area to stay under the radar. The more we had, the more likely we'd be found. "The five of us will go check things out."

"Why should you risk yourselves and not us?" Samuel frowned.

"Because we can hear and smell better than you." Our senses were as strong in human form as in wolf form. It was part of being a shifter. The only advantage our wolf form gave us was in fights, and the whole point of this excursion was to prevent one.

"It'll be fine," Beth said, scanning our surroundings. "We know what we're doing. Just stay put, and we'll be back."

"Maybe I should stay with them." Gabby flinched like she hadn't wanted to say that. "But what if the wolves found them unprotected?"

Dammit, I hadn't even thought of that. "You're right. If you're okay with it, that would be perfect."

Logan's shoulders stiffened, but he didn't say anything.

He couldn't be thrilled with her staying back, but we would all have to be okay with our mates being in danger.

"Let's go." It sucked that we weren't a pack, so mind linking wasn't possible. There were several reasons to stay in human form; we could use hand gestures, and our wolf scent wasn't as strong in human form.

The four of us moved faster without the witches. I continued to follow the tug to the girl. If The Hallowed Guild was already there, they'd be tracking the same person.

I tapped into my wolf, allowing her to surge forward, and then tapped into my animal senses. At the first sign of the enemy, we'd have to stop and regroup.

Enemy.

The word sat heavy in my stomach. I'd never expected to one day consider other wolf shifters my enemies. Hell, I hadn't even considered the Murphy pack my true enemy, more like misguided idiots. Maybe the Rogers pack had had it right all along.

A breeze picked up, blowing toward us, and the faint scent of wolf stopped me dead in my tracks. I detected at least ten individual scents if not more. *Shit, we found them.*

I turned toward the group and pointed to my nose. If we could smell them, then they could potentially hear us. I pointed back in the direction from where we'd come.

Do they have the marked girl? Aidan's concern flew through our bond.

No. I only smell males. At least, that was some good news. *So they haven't caught her... not yet anyway.* We just needed to give them a wide berth.

At least, one thing is on our side. His eyes were still focused on our surroundings.

Beth spun on her heel and led us back to the witches.

When the four of them came into view, my heart calmed.

"Did you find anything?" Gabby spoke more loudly than I'd have liked.

I forced myself not to scold her, but that didn't stop Aidan.

He lifted his finger to his lips. "Shh."

"There are at least ten wolves over there." They were directly to the right of where we probably would've driven through. "But I don't think they are near the witches. The tug was in the opposite direction."

"The perimeter spell should hide the witches from the wolves." Amethyst bit her bottom lip. "Which would mean they know someone is tracking them."

"But how would they know ..." Unless ...

"The girl might know they're hunting her, which means she could be part of The Hallowed Guild." Aidan's jaw clenched.

"You know how to get there, right?" Amethyst would need to help us locate the coven.

"Yes, but it'll be harder since we aren't on a road. I think we should rely on the connection you and Gabby have to her. The perimeter spell won't dampen it, so if you follow the tug, we could get there faster." Amethyst placed her hands on my shoulders. "It'll be fine."

"Do you think they know shifters are hunting them?" I hated the idea that the girl and coven thought they were safe.

"If they have a perimeter spell up, I'm thinking they're aware." Coral tapped her chin. "That could be why they didn't want us coming here."

"So, maybe they were being protective instead of rude." Samuel looked at the ground. "This keeps getting crazier."

"Now, that's something I can agree with." Logan nodded. "The longer we're out here, the more likely they may stumble upon us."

"Especially given the fact that our scents intermingle with theirs now since we found them." Aidan turned toward me. "We need to get moving."

"We also need to stay slow and quiet." Hopefully, the witches would understand this was important. "It's not the coven we need to worry about right now; it's the wolves."

"Got it." Amethyst glanced at the others. "We understand."

"Gabby and I will hang back." Logan touched her arm, tugging her behind Samuel.

It was odd that she didn't put up a fight.

"And I'll be in the middle in case they try to attack from either side." Beth wedged herself between Coral and Amethyst.

"Good, it's settled." I hurried back in the direction of the tug, making sure to stay clear of the other wolves' scents.

The forest was still quiet—like something bad hovered over us. My nerves were on edge, which didn't do me any favors. I worked to calm my ass down.

With each tree I passed, I waited to hear something, anything that would alert us to what was right in front of us.

Are you okay? Aidan's concerned voice popped into my head. *Is something wrong?*

No, I'm being ridiculous. I'd never been afraid of the woods. I'd always felt like a part of them, but things were different. I didn't know what I was a part of now, only that destiny had chosen me—rather, me and four other girls—to right the wrongs from so many damn years ago.

You're not being silly. Aidan sighed behind me. *Your*

world got turned upside down, and you haven't had time to process.

Maybe. But it didn't matter. There were more important things at play than my feelings.

A new musky scent hit my nose. I didn't know why, but I hadn't been prepared for it. I'd hoped we were in the clear. *Aidan, there's a wolf close by.*

It was faint, but with each step, the scent got stronger.

We have to continue. There's no choice. We have to get to the girl. Aidan inhaled sharply behind me. *It's only one wolf.*

Until he alerts the others. I stopped and turned around, making sure Beth, Logan, and Gabby were on the same page.

Their eyes met mine, and they nodded.

Well, okay then. I continued forward, breathing rapidly.

"We're almost there," Amethyst whispered. "I can get us through the perimeter."

She fucking spoke. What the hell was she thinking?

I tensed, waiting. The wolf was close enough to have heard her, and it must be on its way to find us. We'd lost our advantage of being downwind.

I pressed forward because why the hell not at this point. I picked up the pace, hoping to get through the perimeter before the wolf caught up with us. Silence was no longer a priority.

The pounding of paws against the forest floor raced toward us. It didn't give a damn that it was outnumbered. It was running, tearing through the woods.

A brown wolf jumped through the trees, its eyes locking on me.

"We're here." Amethyst pushed past Aidan, not realizing that a wolf stood only five feet away. Her eyes turned toward me, and she froze the moment she saw the wolf. "Shit."

"Go work on the perimeter," Aidan called to her. "We'll hold him off."

As soon as the words were spoken, the wolf hunkered, ready to fight. It lunged right at me, aiming for my neck. It was going for the kill.

I spun to the side, and it only caught air.

It stumbled as it landed on its feet, and Logan punched it in the snout.

A loud whimper escaped the wolf, and blood poured from its nose and into its mouth. Its nearly green eyes glowed as it bared its teeth at us.

"How's it going over there?" Gabby snapped.

"I need more time." Amethyst flinched but continued to work.

The wolf dug its paws into the ground and opened its mouth to bite Logan's arm. I kicked the wolf, nailing it in the side before it could clamp down.

"Don't hurt my mate," Gabby growled as she ran straight toward the animal.

When she was only two feet away, the wolf dropped to the ground. She tripped and fell to her knees. It rounded, its focus back on me.

The wolf jumped, and Aidan sprang forward and knocked the animal out of the air. It hit the ground with a thud.

Amethyst was holding her hands up against an invisible wall, speaking quickly and silently.

Coral and Samuel joined her in the spell.

Hopefully, their combined efforts would allow us through soon.

The wolf got back on its feet and growled. His eyes went straight to the witches.

That was strange. Why would he focus on them instead of us?

It ran toward the witches as their backs were to it.

No, they trusted us to protect them. I tried to be patient and waited for it to lunge. It leaped into the air, and I tapped into my wolf and charged toward it. I planned to steamroll him into the invisible wall, but as we collided, we both blew past the witches and into the protected area.

Great. I'd just let in a wolf the witches were hiding from. This would go over so well.

CHAPTER FOURTEEN

I tumbled over the wolf and landed right on my chest. I struggled to catch my breath as I rolled onto my feet, ready for the wolf to attack again.

But the wolf wasn't interested in me. It stood, glancing around the place.

The rest of my group hurried through the perimeter, and Aidan raced over to me. *Are you okay?* He bent down next to me and brushed my blonde hair out of my face.

Logan, Gabby, and Beth raced straight to the wolf and pinned it to the ground. Logan held the wolf's head steady as Beth and Gabby each grabbed its legs.

Yeah, I am. I forced myself to inhale, and pain throbbed slightly in my chest. Luckily, I'd be healed in a few minutes since it wasn't a serious injury.

What the hell were you doing?

He better be glad he'd asked with concern, or I would've been pissed off right now. *I was trying to smash him into the perimeter wall.* Okay, it sounded stupid when I actually said the words.

Footsteps pounded as nine witches headed in our direction.

A woman in her forties stepped in front of the other eight, and her sable eyes focused on the wolf. Her caramel hair cascaded down her shoulders and back, emphasizing her forest green sweater. Her face turned pink with anger. "What the hell do you think you're doing?"

"We needed to talk to you." Amethyst straightened her shoulders as she met the priestess head-on.

"You're Beatrice's kid, aren't you?" The lady frowned as she took in the wolf. "We told you we couldn't entertain you on this visit."

I couldn't let Amethyst go down for this. "Look, we didn't mean to come here."

"Oh, really?" The lady turned her attention to me. "You just happened to stumble upon us?"

"Actually, yes." *Here it goes.* "We were led here."

"By GPS?" She crossed her arm as sarcasm laced every single word.

"No, by my ..." I wasn't sure what to call it. "... magic?" That had to be the best word for it. I was drawn to these girls, but it was nothing like the mate bond. It was as if we were all interconnected, and hell, we were.

"You don't seem so certain about that," a younger version of the head guard hissed. She stepped up next to the other lady, and I was positive she was her daughter.

Aidan opened his mouth, but considering how much anger was rolling off him, I knew it wasn't wise for him to speak. I grabbed his hand, getting him to help me back to my feet.

"I'm kind of new to magic." If I wanted to be treated as an equal, I had to play the part.

The older witch glared at me. "Obviously. You allowed a mutt to come through the perimeter with you."

"Can't you tell, Mother?" The daughter stepped closer to me. "She's a mutt herself."

"We prefer the term *wolf shifter*," Logan growled as he kept the wolf's head locked in place.

"Not only did we not welcome you here, but you brought wolves with you?" The older witch's hands shook with rage.

"Look, Tabatha, we aren't here to cause any problems." Amethyst's face was drawn, which I'd never seen before.

"Like Emma said, we didn't purposely come here." Coral stood next to her friend, ready to take the coven on. "We were brought here."

The older lady laughed. "The Hallowed Guild? You had to bring them right to us?"

Samuel looked at her like she had two heads. "What? No."

"I have reason to believe you have a hybrid here." This whole situation was getting worse. I took a moment to think of something to calm the hostile atmosphere.

The wolf growled and began fighting to get out of their grips.

"Look, you need to leave." Tabatha crossed her arms and glanced over one shoulder and then the other. "Now."

Okay, maybe that wasn't the best way to go about it. I hadn't meant to make them feel threatened.

"We came here in peace." Aidan lifted his hands and moved toward them as the seven witches behind them lifted their hands, ready to use magic.

"Then why are you here?" Tabatha narrowed her eyes at Aidan. "You have five seconds to tell us before we unleash our magic."

"I'm one of the prophesied girls." I decided to lay it all out on the table before I lost my chance.

Emma, that wolf could be part of The Hallowed Guild. Aidan turned his head so the wolf was in his view. *He could be relaying everything back to his other pack members.*

I get it, but what the hell are we supposed to do? We couldn't leave here empty-handed. They wouldn't listen to us again. *We've come this far. We have to finish it.*

Fine.

The daughter rolled her eyes. "You really expect us to believe that?"

"Salem, let her talk," Tabatha scolded.

Salem's mouth dropped open. "Are you serious?"

Salem? Really? Aidan's voice held a chuckle. *That's so fucking unoriginal.*

I mashed my lips together, trying not to smile.

"Let them talk." Tabatha's words were short and direct as she pointed to me. "Proceed."

"Gabby," I said as I motioned to Gabby, who was holding the wolf's back two paws, "and I are two of the five."

Logan growled, making it quite clear that he wasn't happy that I'd included Gabby in my story.

"Those are some ballsy revelations." She flapped her hands. "How do you plan on proving them?"

"May I show you my mark?" I lifted my hands in surrender. "I promise as soon as you're satisfied, I'll come right back over here."

Emma ...Aidan's warning rang clearly.

Stay ready in case I need you. I didn't say that to comfort him. I really meant it. I was taking a risk, but I had to.

"Fine, approach slowly." Tabatha glanced behind her at the witches. "Keep an eye on her."

"Why the hell do you think we would attack you?" Coral wrinkled her nose.

"Because you brought three witches, apparently two wolf-witches, and four wolves"—Salem pointed at her—"after we said we couldn't host you."

"In all fairness, we didn't mean to bring him." Beth lifted the wolf's paws as if to prove her point.

If a witch coven hadn't been semi threatening us, I'd have burst out laughing. The poor wolf looked ridiculous.

"I'm not sure if that helps our case," Coral huffed.

I slowly walked over to the witches, head bowed slightly to look less threatening. I stopped a foot away and forced myself to turn my back to them, moving my hair to the side. I moved my lobe for a clearer view, so hopefully, they could see my birthmark from where they stood.

"Holy shit," Tabatha breathed, her body tense and jaw set. "She has the whole damn pentagram."

"Are you sure it's real?" Salem stepped up next to her mom to see for herself.

"It looks just like Ivory's ... except hers is only one point." Tabatha blinked like she was still in denial.

"I bet the girl you're protecting has the lower right side of the star." If Gabby's was the upper right, it made sense for us to be finding the girls in order.

The older witch beside Tabatha gasped. "How do you know that? That's not possible."

"It's going in clockwise order of the pentagram vertices." In order to gain their trust, I would be open with them so they would take me to the girl.

"That makes sense." Tabatha nodded as she rubbed her thumb along her bottom lip.

"Last question. If he isn't with you," Salem said,

gesturing to the detained wolf, "why the hell did you bring him in here with you?"

Aidan made his way to my side and took my hand. "He attacked us at the perimeter's edge. My mate was protecting the witches while they took down the perimeter for us. She accidentally brought him in with us."

That was better than telling them I'd been planning to use their spell wall as a strategic advantage that had backfired ... maybe.

"Great, so one of the destined can't even protect their own kind." Salem tipped her face toward the sky and closed her eyes.

"She's both witch and wolf." Beth chuckled, enjoying ruffling their feathers.

That's why I loved her most of the time. "In all fairness, I didn't even know about this until three weeks ago, and I'm doing the best I can. I will say, we got here and found you."

"Touché." Tabatha grinned. "Go get Ivory, Vlad."

"Yes, Priestess." The tallest among the seven on the end bowed his head, his stark-white hair falling over his shoulders. "I'll be right back." He headed toward where the trees were thinner, where I assumed their houses must be.

The older woman scowled. "So, what are we going to do with that mutt?"

That was an excellent question for which I didn't know the answer. "It's odd. He wasn't with the larger pack that we smelled on our way in."

"Maybe they split up to cover more ground?" Logan's white eyes met mine. "There's no telling what all he's sharing with them right now."

He's right. Aidan faced the wolf behind us. *Killing him as quick as possible is in our best interest.*

I don't know. Something felt off. *I'm not sure that's the right call.*

"Of course he needs to die," a coven member called from the back.

"I think we should learn what he knows." If for no other reason, that would buy us more time. "If we could learn more about his pack and what they're looking for, it would at least put us on the right path."

"I agree with Emma." Amethyst sighed. "He's worried, not angry or malicious."

Tabatha gazed at her. "How do you know that?"

"I'm an empath."

"Those are rare," Salem whispered. "I didn't know there was one close by."

"We don't broadcast my gifts much." Amethyst walked over to stand on my other side. "I agree that we should determine what he knows."

"Fine." Tabatha nodded. "Salem, show those three to the barn in the back. Force his shift and get him clothed. Secure him, and then let me know when to make our way down there."

"Yes, Mother." Salem turned and waved Logan, Gabby, and Beth on. "Bring him this way."

"This will be fun," Gabby grumbled. "How are we going to carry him?"

"Easy." Logan secured his arm around the wolf's neck and applied pressure. The wolf was soon passed out cold.

Beth let go of its paws and stood, stretching out her arms. "Damn, my back hurts." She cringed. "I sound like a middle-aged human."

Logan tossed the wolf over his shoulder and followed Salem.

"Yeah, you do." Gabby stood and dusted off her knees.

"I'm still going with you, but Beth can stay back." She jogged to catch up with them.

"Sounds like a plan," Beth replied.

"While they're doing this, let's go meet Vlad halfway." Tabatha motioned for the witches behind her to turn. "There's no reason to turn you away now that you're here."

That doesn't sound very nice. I guessed we should be glad she was being honest, though.

No, but they aren't watching our every move, so that's progress. Aidan tugged on my hand as we followed behind them.

Our group moved in silence, and I was taken aback when we stepped out from the trees. Their space was massive, and they had made the land into a farm. About thirty houses lined the enormous gardens. The houses weren't large but small and sturdy. The windows were open, and the curtains blew in the breeze.

On our left were herb and vegetable gardens. Rows of corn, carrots, radishes, and several other vegetables grew. Twenty people were out, working in the fields.

Beyond the gardens, horses, goats, cows, and chickens ran rampant in a large fenced-in area.

Logan, Gabby, and Salem were already halfway to the barn. It was almost humorous to watch Logan carry the wolf as if it weighed nothing at all.

"That right there is where she's staying." Tabatha pointed at the third house down. The front door opened, revealing a tall young woman around my age. Her hair was a dark brown, close to the color of tree bark, and contrasted against her pale white skin.

Now, her name, Ivory, made sense.

Vlad stepped out behind her, and they headed in our direction.

"Let's wait for them here," Tabatha commanded. "They'll be ready for us at the barn shortly."

We all stopped and watched as they approached us.

The girl wore a long gray dress that hung loosely across her thin body. Her hair blew behind her as she walked, brushing the small of her back. Her eyes settled directly onto mine.

A prickling spread over me as she neared. It was the tug but amplified tenfold.

She stopped and bowed her head slightly at Tabatha. "You summoned me?" Her quiet voice shocked me since she had a strong wolf inside. It was easy to feel her power.

"Yes, dear. It seems we have a big surprise." Tabatha touched her shoulder. "Two of the girls came looking for you."

Her brows furrowed. "I don't understand."

I linked with Aidan, concerned that Ivory might not take this well. *And I always thought you were blunt.*

"Hi, Ivory. I'm Emma." I reached out my hand, and when we touched, our connection sparked between us.

She jerked her hand out of mine and took a step back.

"This is my mate, Aidan, and my other friends." I introduced our group, one by one.

"You're a half witch and shifter like me." Hope sprang in her eyes. "I thought I was alone and would be killed."

"Well, you definitely aren't alone." I turned my head and moved my hair so she could see my mark. "There is another girl here who has one too."

"Mom, we're ready," Salem hollered from the barn. "You better hurry. He's getting testy."

That wasn't good. I took off for the barn with Aidan and Beth right by my side. The barn hadn't been painted in a long time, but as we got closer, I noticed specks of white paint.

"Calm down." Logan's loud, growly voice could be heard strong and clear. "And if you hurt her, I will kill you."

I'd thought the wolf would be unconscious like Logan and Gabby had been back at the other coven.

We rushed into the barn, and the smell of hay and manure hit me hard in the chest. Stables lined the aisle on either side, but straight at the back, centered against the wall, was the wolf in man form. They'd put a cloth over his bottom half, but his chest and legs were bare. He had dark olive skin, and blood trickled from his wrists and ankles where rope restrained him. His brown hair hung in his face, and dark green eyes were filled with hate. He was almost as large as Aidan. A growl thundered from his chest.

"Oh my God." Ivory's voice was barely a whisper. "Remus?"

My head jerked in her direction, and I took in her horrified expression. She knew the wolf that the witches planned to kill.

CHAPTER FIFTEEN

"Ivory?" Remus stilled in his seat, his eyes on her. "Is that you?"

"Of course it is." She hurried over to him. "Why is he tied up?"

"Because he attacked them while they were looking for you." Salem motioned to me.

Her brows furrowed. "Why did you attack them?"

"I thought they were coming here to hurt you." His face creased with pain. "I was going out of my mind, searching for you." He paused and his shoulders stiffened. "Are they forcing you to stay here?"

"What?" Ivory shook her head hard. "No. You know why I'm here."

He lowered his voice as if to keep everyone from hearing. "You know witches can't be trusted."

"This is a common mantra that I don't like," Samuel grumbled. "I've never hurt anyone who hasn't asked for it."

"Define 'asked for it,'" Logan snarled.

"We are all on the same team." This shit was getting on

my nerves. There was only so much drama I could handle. "So, remember that, or you can't be part of this adventure."

"I go where she goes." Logan flinched under my gaze.

"Not necessarily. She has to stay with us because I won our fight." Winning our fight had given me this advantage, and the advantage was the only reason I'd been willing to risk losing. "You weren't part of the agreement."

You amazing, sneaky woman. Aidan chuckled in my mind. *You found a loophole and have leverage.*

That wasn't my intention, but I'll use it if needed. I lifted my chin and met her gaze dead-on. "Do you understand?"

"She's right." Gabby glanced at her mate. "I won't leave her even if you do."

Logan scowled.

Remus sniffed the air. "You smell like a shifter. Why are you protecting the witches?"

"The same reason Ivory ran here for protection." That had to be why she'd come here.

"They've been hiding me from our pack." Ivory touched her left ear. "You know why."

"Then, let's run away together." Remus leaned forward, but when the ropes kept his arms in place, he jerked back.

"I can't put you in harm's way. You're the alpha heir." Ivory licked her lips and touched his shoulder. "Go back to the pack before you get labeled as a traitor."

His shoulders stiffened. "I can't."

"Who the hell is this?" Tabatha walked over to Ivory and crossed her arms.

"He's my ..." Ivory trailed off.

"Let me guess ... mate." Beth smirked.

Ivory's mouth dropped open. "How did you know?"

"Just a guess." Beth turned to me. "I'm seeing some similarities here."

I couldn't argue there. "Why are you running from your pack?" I already knew the answer, but I didn't want to assume anything.

Remus narrowed his eyes at me. "Don't tell her."

"Then, let me guess: The Hallowed Guild," Coral spat the words in disgust.

Ivory cringed. "Is it that obvious? I thought it was a secret."

"Because they," I said, pointing to Aidan then Logan, "were members too."

"That makes no sense." Ivory pivoted toward us. "Then, why are they with you if you're one of the chosen too?"

"Wait ..." Beth lifted a hand to me and pouted. "I already answered that ... mates."

"At least, for the three of us, our mates were part of the Hallowed Guild." The original witch had a sick sense of humor. Would all five of us be that way?

"It doesn't matter." Ivory straightened her shoulders as she faced her mate. "You need to hurry before it's too late."

Remus lifted his chin. "I already told you I can't."

"Why?" Ivory threw her hands to the side.

"Because they're hunting you." He leaned forward enough so the ropes wouldn't hurt him. "I can't let that happen."

"We'll take care of her." Gabby glanced at him. "So you don't need to worry."

"Actually, we're the ones taking care of her." Salem grabbed a shovel from the ground and stepped toward Remus. "We found her in the woods, and we stopped because we recognized our coven energy coming from her.

Mom recognized her immediately. She's my aunt's daughter, and we protect our own."

"I understand wanting to protect your family and coven, but if she doesn't come with us to find the others, the prophecy won't be fulfilled." Did they really think we'd come all this way just to take a glance at her and be on our merry way? "We need her to find the fourth and fifth girls."

"Wait ... are both of you like me?" Ivory's eyes widened as her focus flicked from me and then to Gabby.

"Yes." I hoped that comforted her.

"My mark appeared right after that huge-ass earthquake. It scared me." Gabby rubbed her hands along her arms.

"The same thing happened to me." A small frown appeared on Ivory's face. "I mean, I'm exactly what I was raised to hate. The morning when I saw this ... curse ..." She trailed off.

"I still can't believe you were a member of The Hallowed Guild." I didn't know why, but her being part of the pack shocked the hell out of me.

Her shoulders sagged. "As much as any woman can be."

"What does that even mean?" Amethyst leaned against a stall door. She looked worn down, probably because of the charged energy in the room. Being an empath had to be exhausting, especially in times like these.

"I mean, The Hallowed Guild think that women are too weak and unworthy to lead." Ivory chewed on her bottom lip. "So do you really think we're a huge part of the society and pack? It's more like we take care of things at home and serve our men."

"What is it, the twenties?" Coral gagged. "That's disgusting. A woman leader is stronger in ways a man could never be. That's one reason I love being a witch."

"Either way, it's kind of sexist." If both groups only had one sex leading all the time, there was no way that the best leader could be chosen each time.

Gabby sighed. "We aren't here to debate that."

She was right. It wasn't important right now. "Look, Ivory, we came here to find you," I said, laying my cards out on the table. "We need you to come with us so we can finish what the original witch started."

"Like hell she is." Remus yanked against the rope again. "She'll be more of a target than she is here with the witches. The pack is tracking her scent and waiting for someone to leave."

Great, so the longer we stayed here, the likelier it was that they'd pick up our scents and spread out. For once, it'd be nice if something wound up being easy.

"There's no reason to leave." Vlad motioned to the front of the barn. "We have everything we need to survive here."

"Are you actually saying you don't want us to fulfill the prophecy?" It surprised me, to say the least.

"Four other girls came before, and none of them succeeded." Salem picked at her fingers, feigning disinterest in the conversation. "So, I don't see why you all think you're any different."

"So, the chosen witch set off a massive earthquake, causing the mark to appear on four others?" From what Beatrice had told us, it had never gotten that far.

"No, this is the furthest one has come." Tabatha ran her hands through her hair.

"Really?" Ivory focused on me. "So we might stand a chance."

"Mom." Salem dropped her hands. "What are you doing?"

"Aren't you tired of hiding?" Amethyst motioned to

Remus. "And being afraid that the next wolf you come across might kill you? If they succeed, we won't have to worry anymore. The balance will be restored between both races, and we can finally find peace."

"Then, the answer is simple." Ivory took in a shaky breath.

"No, no, it's not." Remus's jaw clenched. "Can you untie me? I won't attack anyone."

"How can we be sure?" Salem tilted her head.

Aidan leaned back on his heels. "Because we'd smell it if he was lying."

"And he means it." Amethyst nodded. "I can feel it."

Wow, Salem had some serious anger issues. I had a feeling I didn't want to know what had made her that way.

"Fine." Tabatha marched over to Remus and pulled a knife from her pocket.

"What are you doing?" Salem asked in horror as her mom cut the man free.

"We aren't barbarians." Tabatha stepped back and put the knife back in her pocket. "If he isn't a risk to us, we don't need to treat him like one."

"Uh ... thanks." Remus stood and held the piece of cloth in front of him.

"You didn't think that through, did you?" Beth snorted. His front side was covered, but his ass was bare for all of us to see.

"Uh ... not exactly." He cleared his throat and stared at the ground. "Does anyone have some pants I can borrow?"

"Yeah." Vlad lifted a finger. "I'll be right back." The older man hurried off to his house.

"Maybe you should sit back down?" Beth smirked and waggled her brows.

A low growl came from Ivory. If she hadn't already shared that he was her mate, I'd have known for sure now.

Look at the reserved girl ready to take Beth down. Aidan wrapped an arm around me. *Honestly, I bet you Ivory could take her.*

I don't know. Beth is a badass in her own right. I diverted my eyes from Remus, not needing another full moon sighting in broad daylight.

"Fine." He sat and rearranged the cloth to cover his jewels. "But I'm serious. We need to get out of here and hide."

"Your father will find us." Ivory placed a hand on her heart. "I couldn't forgive myself if something happened to you."

"Dammit, you're more important." His brown hair fell into his eyes, but he ignored it.

"All right." Ivory gave him a small smile. "I want you by my side. Honestly, I'm not sure I could handle being that far away from you."

"I'm glad we agree." Remus stood again, forgetting all about his naked ass, and pressed his lips to hers. "We're in this together ... forever."

The fact that they'd gotten this right compared to my tumultuous past with Aidan warmed my heart. I was glad they weren't fighting their bond.

She pulled back and placed a hand on his chest. "We should be careful, though, with you being a rogue. I'm only half-wolf, so I shouldn't struggle like you."

"It's been hard, but I'm still standing." He lowered his face to catch her downcast eyes.

"What?" She sucked in a breath and took a step back. "What are you saying?"

"I feel like we're watching a romance story," Beth whispered to Samuel.

"Right, like, bring out the popcorn." Samuel pretended to wipe away a tear. "Now don't get me wrong, I like action flicks, but sincere romances like this make my eyes water."

I think we've all lost our minds. It was almost like Beth and Samuel were living in a different world at times.

"He has obviously left the pack." Salem shifted her weight to one leg.

"Well, then, it's settled. You're coming with us." Remus knew how the pack thought and would give us an advantage. "We can leave now and get back on the road."

"We swore to protect her, so that's a no-go." Salem placed her hands on her hips and faced me. "You can't just waltz in here unannounced and take my cousin."

"Yes, she can, and she will." Tabatha locked eyes with me.

"What? No." Salem stomped on the ground like a toddler. "What the hell are you doing?"

"We're prisoners here." Tabatha waved her hands around the barn. "Yes, we may have everything we need, but it's largely due to The Hallowed Guild pack living right next door and harassing us every damn time we try to leave our home."

"But Mom ..."

"There aren't any buts, Salem." Tabatha flapped her arms. "Like Emma said, this is the furthest any chosen has come to ending this. Do you really want to prevent our race from living in peace with wolves?"

The fact that the witches wouldn't fight us on this any longer lifted some of the anxiety from my shoulders.

"Well, I'm in." Ivory nodded in my direction. "Yes, I've

been raised to think of our kind as abominations, but it's clear that needs to change."

Footsteps entered the barn, and Vlad returned with a pair of sweatpants. He threw them at Remus. "These should work."

Remus caught them and pointed at a stall. "I'll go change in there."

"Please, do." Tabatha nodded as Remus passed her and went into the stall on the left.

"Did anyone think to bring the map?" None of us was carrying a bag, so I doubted it.

"No, we'll have to do the locator spell when we get back into town." Amethyst glanced at Salem, hinting that she didn't trust her. "Let's focus on getting back to the vehicles."

I didn't trust her either, so at least, that was one thing we had in common. Salem was angry and not a fan of ours.

"That's going to be tricky," Remus said as he walked out of the stall. Thankfully, I could look at him again without feeling like a pervert. "The wolves are hanging out off to the east."

"That's why we came across you instead." Aidan stuck his hands inside his jeans pockets.

"They rotate." Remus walked over to Ivory and took her hand in his. The cuts on his wrists were already healing due to his wolf shifter blood.

"Do we need to leave from the other side?" Logan stiffened. "We've only been here a few hours."

"I'm not sure. They're purposely keeping their run random." Remus frowned. "That's how they work. It's so no one can pin their next move."

"So we make a break for it and hope for the best?" I'd been foolish to think we could just retrace our steps.

"No, we leave the same way we came here." Aidan

formed his hands into a steeple. "Let's leave farther to the west than where we came in and use our noses from there."

"We can lower the perimeter in sections until you find a safe spot." Tabatha hurried to Ivory and gave her a large hug. "It was nice to have you as part of our family for a week. Your mother would be so proud of the woman you've become."

"Thank you." Ivory hugged the witch back with such fierceness. "I hope I can come back someday. Seeing those pictures and her drawings meant more to me than you'll ever know."

"We really need to go." Remus surveyed us. "The longer we take, the likelier they'll come across us."

"Then, there's no time to waste," Aidan said as he took my hand, and our group headed back to the perimeter line.

I hoped we could get back to our cars without a problem.

CHAPTER SIXTEEN

The witches took us farther west along the perimeter.

"This should be safer if they are spreading out," Tabatha said as she faced Ivory. "My dear sweet niece, you better come back to us soon."

"I will." She hugged the priestess hard. "It's amazing that this is the first place I've ever felt truly at home."

"It's because both your halves thrive in nature and your witchy side finally felt accepted." Salem glared at the wolves and witches. "Just remember that no one can come between family."

That sounded like a threat. "You do realize we're not trying to take her from you?" She reminded me of Finn—brimming with anger.

"That's not what it looks like from here," she snarled. "Our coven grows smaller each year, and you're taking away one of the few family members we have left."

Amethyst grimaced. "Why does it keep growing smaller?"

"Because we've been hiding here for the last fifty years since The Hallowed Guild found our campgrounds and we had to stay protected. There aren't many men to choose from if you know what I mean. Reproduction has stalled since we can't find partners outside of the coven." Tabatha sighed as she pulled back from Ivory. "Say goodbye to your cousin. If we want to survive, she has to go, and they need to succeed."

"Fine, but if something happens to her …" Salem scowled; unhappiness radiating off her. "… I know who to take my anger out on."

"And you mean every single one of us, right?" Aidan stood in front of me and faced off with the witch. "We're a package deal, including your cousin, Ivory."

"Now listen here …" Salem's face turned red.

"No, he's right." Ivory squeezed her cousin before pulling back and standing next to me. "This is what I need to do."

"And nothing is going to happen to her." Remus took his mate's hand. "We already promised ourselves to each other before the earthquake, and nothing will change that, even leaving my father and pack behind."

"Even though you're the alpha's son, they won't hesitate to kill you." Ivory's eyes filled with concern. "Maybe you should go back before it's too late."

"There's no way in hell." Remus planted his feet shoulder length apart, ready to argue. "I'm in this with you like a mate should be."

"He won't change his mind." Amethyst patted Ivory on the arm. "He's resolved."

"Fine." Ivory stood on her tiptoes and kissed him.

"We're killing too much time." Logan's body stiffened, and I wasn't sure he could breathe despite talking. "The longer we're here, the harder it'll be to get back to the Suburbans."

"He's right." Aidan took my hand and tugged me to the perimeter. "Emma and I will take the lead."

"Then, Amethyst can follow behind you, and I'll go next." Beth lifted her hand, volunteering.

"Okay, I'll be behind Beth." Coral turned to the remaining wolves. "Who's going to be between me and Samuel?"

"I'm thinking those two." Remus pointed at Logan and Gabby. "Ivory and I will take up the rear. We know the woods better and can watch your backs."

That didn't sit well with me. *Do you think they'll try to sneak off?*

Not sure. Aidan frowned. "Is that wise?"

"They're both committed to the cause." Amethyst squinted as she read their true intent. "If something changes, I'll let you know."

"But—" Logan growled, but Coral lifted her hand, cutting him off.

"Amethyst will feel the change before they've even processed it." Coral crossed her arms as if daring the wolf. "So, it's fine."

"It'll be okay." Gabby touched his arm.

Logan rolled his shoulders and took a deep breath. "Fine, but if they double-cross us, there's no one to blame but yourself."

"This sounds like another common mantra." Beth exhaled with annoyance. "At some point, when the same threat is repeated over and over, it loses its meaning."

She had an excellent point. "We need to focus on the goal. It's not like we can find one of the chosen again if something does happen."

Salem's forehead wrinkled. "What do you mean?"

Don't tell her anything. Aidan's face was unreadable despite the anxiety coursing through our bond.

I hoped I could hide my real feelings like him. Otherwise, everyone would know I wasn't confident. "It means we need to get moving before the Guild catches us."

Salem narrowed her eyes at me but kept her mouth shut.

"We'll take the perimeter down." Tabatha walked over to the invisible wall and began murmuring words.

Vlad hurried to stand next to her, stepping right into the chant alongside her.

"It's down." Tabatha motioned to the forest. "But you need to move so we can put it back up. They'll be on us within seconds otherwise."

Aidan took off first into the woods. He sniffed the air for enemy scents. *Come on. It's clear for now.*

I motioned for the others to follow, and they lined up in the order we'd discussed.

Our whole group was moving through the trees.

Is everything okay? I was being stupid. He would've told me if it wasn't, but I needed to check. It somehow made me feel more in control.

So far so good. Aidan replied as we continued our steady pace.

The fact that we couldn't run stressed me out, but there wasn't much we could do about it. The witches couldn't move as fast as the wolves, and we had to be slow enough so they could remain silent. If we pushed them, our chances of getting caught would increase tenfold.

I glanced over my shoulder, and everyone was focused straight ahead. Ivory and Remus scanned the area from the back on high alert.

A musky scent hit me. *Aidan.*

Shit, they've been by here recently. Aidan kept his pace steady, but he was on high alert.

I turned to communicate to our group, and it was clear that the wolves behind realized the same thing.

Amethyst's face was paler than normal. She sensed how the wolves felt.

Aidan turned right, trying to lose their scent. Hopefully, they were long gone and wouldn't be doubling back any time soon. However, the more we continued in that direction, the stronger the smell became.

Hurry, let's go in the opposite direction. We were heading straight to them. We'd assumed they would still be hanging out where they'd been earlier, and we'd been wrong ... I just prayed we hadn't been dead wrong.

Aidan pivoted, leading us to the left, and he picked up the pace.

Slow down. I said, feeling the panic wafting off him. For the first time ever, he wasn't thinking clearly. *They'll hear us if you push Amethyst, Coral, and Samuel too hard.*

Dammit, you're right. He replied as he slowed, allowing us to catch up to him. *I just have a bad feeling about this.*

Take a deep breath and keep moving forward. That's all we could do. If the Guild attacked us, we'd deal with it just like we had been doing. *The closer we get to the vehicles, the less distance we have to fight.*

With each step, paranoia filled me even more. It had to be Aidan's mixing with my own fear. It didn't matter though. I forced myself to tap into nature to help calm my ridden nerves.

A branch snapped less than a mile from us. A sound parallel to a train headed right in our direction. They'd picked up our scent.

Run, I shouted the words in my mind at Aidan. The scents were getting stronger, so we had nothing left to lose.

Aidan increased his speed, and soon, our group of ten was running with abandon through the woods. It didn't matter that our feet pounded against the ground; they'd already found us.

My ears perked as I heard paws digging into the ground, rushing to get to us.

"They're here," Amethyst breathed.

I almost snapped, "No shit,' but she could've been talking to Coral and Samuel for all I knew, so I bit back the words.

Luckily, we're only a mile away from the vehicles. Aidan kept charging forward. *Keep this pace until we have to stop. The closer we are, the better.*

Witches could run fast, albeit not as fast as wolves.

The volume of our breathing competed with our running footsteps as adrenaline fueled our bodies. Just when the trees began to thin out and the vehicles came into view, three wolves sprang into our path.

None of us slowed as we pushed to reach the vehicles. However, the wolves were gaining ground.

Coral spun and lifted her hands and made a tree fall squarely in front of the wolves. The wolves jumped over the trunk like it was nothing.

"You three need to back down," Remus ordered the three wolves, his words laced with alpha will, but they didn't pause.

"Since you left the pack, they don't consider you their alpha heir anymore." Ivory pushed her legs, her long hair flying behind her like a cape.

The wolves were only ten feet away, which meant we needed to turn around and fight.

Aidan reached back and placed the keys in my hand. *Get everyone else in the car while we fight them off. Honk once you're settled, and I'll make my way to you.*

I wanted to argue, but he was right. We needed to hurry and stay together in case more wolves appeared.

"Come on, let's keep going." I waved the group behind me on and ran even harder.

I turned around to see Aidan, Logan, and Remus taking on the three wolves. Of course, the three of them would. *You better be safe.*

All three of us are former Hallowed Guild members. We know how they fight better than anyone else here. Aidan cut our connection off as a wolf lunged at him.

I stopped in my tracks, and right as I began heading back, Amethyst grabbed my arm.

"We have to get in the car." Amethyst shook me gently. "You going back there will only prolong this."

Dammit. How did she know that? Miserable empath.

It took all my self-control to turn around and rush back to the Suburban. Everything in me told me to go help my mate, but what if I caused him to get hurt?

The wolves tried to get past the three men, but they were holding their own. Cries and whimpers came from the enemy wolves.

The dirt ground blended with gravel. My hands shook as I mashed the UNLOCK button repeatedly. *That son of a bitch better be unlocked when we get there.*

The other vehicle honked, alerting me that Samuel had done the same thing. When we reached the Suburban, I went to the driver's side, yanked the door open, and climbed in. Beth ran with the witches to the other vehicle as the hybrid girls piled in with me.

I honked the horn several times and linked with Aidan. *We're in.*

Remus squatted, and as the wolf jumped at him, he stood, swinging his hands up and right into the wolf's neck. The gray wolf flipped in the air and landed hard on its back.

He turned and ran to Aidan, who was fighting a wolf on its hind legs. The wolf was swinging its paws and trying to sink its claws into my mate's skin.

The moment I was about to get out, Remus punched the wolf hard in the head. The wolf's head wobbled before it fell over.

Thank God. I sagged against the steering wheel. I'd really thought that Aidan might get hurt.

The two of them reached Logan right as he head-butted the wolf. He then picked the animal up and threw it fifteen feet away.

Aidan linked with me as the three of them took off toward us. *Start the car.*

Seeing him run toward me broke me out of whatever torture spell I'd been in. I stuck the key in the ignition and started the car. "Open the back door."

Ivory sat in the middle seat facing the woods. She flung the door open and jumped into the back on the driver's side.

I leaned over the center console, ignoring the pain that erupted from my side, and pushed open the huge-ass door.

The three men were running at full speed as the three wolves chased them down.

As soon as my ass hit my seat again, Aidan jumped into the front passenger seat as the other two large men climbed in the back.

Tires squealed as Samuel burned out of our spot, getting out of my way.

Even before the doors were shut, I pressed the gas hard.

The back end of the car swung to the side, and the wheels spat up gravel. One of the wolves lunged for us, the car jerked forward, and I spun onto the road.

Samuel raced back toward town, and I stayed right behind him. In the side mirror, I saw the wolves running as hard as they could to keep up with us.

"Let's get to town fast," Aidan said, his raspy voice fueling my anxiety even more.

A few cars passed us, heading in the opposite direction. It would at least give the wolves pause before they did something stupid.

Logan hunkered and headed in the backseat to sit on the side, putting Gabby in the center. Beyond that, no one else made a noise.

"They're stopping," Gabby called from the backseat. "Why?"

"My father must be summoning them." Remus pulled himself into the seat Ivory had been sitting in. "They're regrouping to hunt us."

"Well, it's a good thing we won't be here when they do." We needed to pull over and perform the spell to find out where our next location was. We didn't need to hang out in this city longer than we had to. *Watch and make sure the wolves aren't following us. When we're cleared, let's stop.*

Okay. Aidan's eyes stayed glued to the woods.

Keeping my eyes on the road, I took the phone out of my pocket and hit Beth's name. It rang all of one time before she answered.

"Hey."

"We need to stop and figure out our next move." We'd become more of a target if we didn't leave soon. "So we can get on our way out of here."

"I couldn't agree more."

I linked with Aidan. *Is it safe to stop?*

Yeah for a few minutes. Aidan frowned, not thrilled with the idea.

"Can you guys get the map out and pull over somewhere?" My heart was still pounding after what we'd been through.

"Sure. Let me get it all ready, and we'll find somewhere to stop." Beth hung up the phone, and after another couple miles, Samuel pulled over to the side of the road.

Once I'd pulled up behind him and stopped the car, I turned around. "The spell needs to be performed outside, but we should make it quick." There was no telling when the wolves would be searching for us again.

We all climbed out, and Amethyst laid the map on the ground and placed gravel on the corners to prevent the breeze from blowing it away.

"Ivory, we need a drop of your blood for the locator spell." I pointed to me and then Gabby. "If all three of us combine our blood, it'll show us where the fourth girl is."

Remus grimaced and stiffened. "Blood?"

"Oh, stop. Magic comes with a price." Ivory smacked his arm. "Okay, so what do we do?"

"I'll keep watch while you do this." Aidan walked over to the other side of the car, on alert for the wolves.

I bit into my finger just like the previous two times and turned my hand over, letting several drops of blood hit the center of the map. Once again, my blood inched toward where we were now. "That's odd. Why isn't it going to West Virginia?"

"Because Gabby is here with you." Samuel pointed to Gabby. "Your blood leads you to her, and she's here in North Dakota."

Beth nodded. "That makes sense."

Gabby then pierced her fingertip and added her blood to the map. It inched toward North Dakota as well.

"Now it's your turn." I turned around and noticed that Remus had turned pale. He blinked and watched as our blood slid to Jamestown and stopped.

"That's freaky as hell." He shuddered.

"Okay." Ivory bit into her wrist and turned it over, allowing several large drops of her blood to land on the map.

Amethyst spoke a few words that were inaudible, and then our blood headed west on the map.

"It never gets old." Beth snorted as her blue eyes stayed on the map.

The blood left a faint trail behind as it slid across the rest of the United States. It slowed as it made its way to California and stopped right at Ojai.

"There. That's where we go." I couldn't believe this was my first tour of the United States and I couldn't enjoy it.

"Of course it would be twenty-seven hours from here," Coral groaned.

Aidan banged on the car. "I think I see something. Let's hit the road."

He didn't have to tell me twice.

CHAPTER SEVENTEEN

Normally, I'd be complaining about being stuck in the vehicle so damn long, but not this trip. Not after a pack of wolves chased us down. I was enjoying the safety of the car, especially when Aidan took over driving.

We pulled into Ojai three days later, right when we were all becoming super restless. We'd spent the whole day in the car, and it was coming up on eight in the evening. Between the car ride and it being eleven on the east coast, I could barely keep my eyes open.

I'd found a quaint bed-and-breakfast for us to stay at. It was near the wilderness that our girl was probably living in.

The whole town was quaint and gorgeous. The buildings were older but well-kept, and the woods were thick and lush, providing shifters and witches with plenty of room to live in.

We pulled up to a house built on a large hill halfway up a mountain. A beige stone stairwell led to the front porch, and the support columns and window trims were painted white. The front of the house was spotted, and to the right, a large window framed the sunroom.

"This is so stinkin' cute." Ivory's eyes lit up. "It's like the perfect mixture of old with a modern flair."

That was the perfect way to describe it. "We have five rooms reserved here." We had been sharing rooms, but this place only had one bed in each room, with no pull-out couch. However, it was half the price of all the other places we'd stayed at.

Remus shut the door as Aidan popped open the trunk for us to get our stuff.

It wasn't long before the ten of us were heading up the stairs and into the house.

We stepped directly into a living room with white walls. The flooring was maple, and the large stone fireplace matched the front porch. Right atop it was a huge flat-screen with a yellow couch in front of it. On either side of the couch was a brown wicker chair with flowery cushions. The window to the left had matching yellow swagged curtains.

"Welcome." A lady in her mid-forties stepped from the hallway and into the room. Her brown eyes flicked to each one of us, and unease appeared in her eyes. "I'm assuming you're the large group that's staying here for the night."

"Yes." I stepped forward and smiled. "I reserved five rooms."

"Perfect." She waved us on down a hallway to the left.

Aidan adjusted our bag on his shoulder as he came beside me and took my hand. *This looks like a nice place.*

It did, but I'd booked this place for a reason. It was on the outskirts of the small city and right next to the mountains that stretched for miles.

"Okay, this side of the house is all yours." She pointed down the hallway. "There are three rooms to the left and two on the right. Each one has their own bathroom. You can split up however you'd like." She then faced the other way. "The kitchen is right past the living room on the left. There you can access the dining room and the back patio, where you can eat or hang out for leisure."

"From what I remember of the description online, doesn't the back way lead to a hiking area?" That's where I planned for us to take off in the morning. I had a feeling we'd find the third girl there.

"Yes, it does. There is a walkway down the back of the house, and the others will lead you to the trailhead." The lady ran her hand through her purple hair and sighed as her free hand tugged at her green sweater. "But you need to be careful. The wolves are a little more riled up than normal. Hikers have been seeing them more, which is odd. They usually keep to themselves unless they get hungry." She took a few steps away from us.

"We're experienced hikers." Aidan tried to reassure her. "We're equipped to handle all situations."

"You all do seem like you can take care of yourselves, especially those three." She pointed to Aidan, Logan, and Remus.

Yeah, those three dudes were kind of scary, especially when standing next to each other. "Thank you."

"Is there anything else you need?" She smiled, uneasily.

Humans weren't comfortable around us, even if they were drawn to us. It was a weird supernatural thing.

"Nope, we're good." Amethyst gave her a comforting smile.

"Okay. Breakfast will be ready at eight, so if you don't want to miss out, don't be late." She nodded and hurried off, glancing behind at us one more time.

"Well, that wasn't awkward or anything." Beth shifted

her weight to one leg. "So we have five rooms. How are we pairing off?"

"Really? You're actually asking?" Gabby grinned. "If so, dibs on Logan."

The past day, they'd been whispering in the backseat and getting closer. I wasn't surprised she'd been so forward this time.

Logan's eyes widened, though. "Uh ... yeah." Then his mouth stretched into a smirk.

"Well, it's obvious Ivory and I are staying together." Remus brushed Ivory's face with his fingertips.

"Okay, I get all the mates are paired up." Beth placed a hand on her hip. "I was talking more about me and the witches."

"I'm not sleeping with you." Coral shook her head. "You kept me up last night."

"Hey, she's kept me up plenty too," Samuel huffed.

"Dear Goddess, I'll stay with her." Amethyst reached into her purse and pulled out a set of earplugs. "I got these yesterday at Walmart. I figured you guys would force me to sleep with her soon enough."

"Hey, wait." Coral scowled. "There weren't any earplugs there. I looked."

Amethyst grinned. "Because I got to them first."

I rarely saw Amethyst's playful side. She was usually so considerate and busy worrying about everyone else. I liked it.

"Okay, it's solved." Aidan tugged me to the back right bedroom. "We'll take this one here. It should look out over the mountains, so we'll keep an eye out."

"We'll leave it up to you eight on how to separate the remaining rooms." It felt like forever since I'd had alone time with Aidan. Last night, we'd shared a room with

Remus and Ivory. It had been nice and given us a chance to talk face to face, unlike in the Suburban. Granted, we'd all been worn out from a full day of travel.

Aidan and I hurried into the room, and right before the door closed, I heard Coral chuckle. "I wonder what they are hurrying off to do."

Thank God we were already in our room or I'd have died of embarrassment.

I spun around and checked out our room. The room's exterior wall was one large window, and an all-glass door right in front of the bed took us out to our own private table area were we could enjoy the views. A side trail headed down the side of the mountain and connected to the trails.

A large bed with a white comforter sat right in the center. The twinkling lights outside from the patio made the room whimsical and romantic.

"Wow, this is gorgeous." I'd never quite seen a small town like this before.

"Yeah, I'd have to agree." Aidan placed our luggage on the ground and turned toward me. "This would be a great place for a pack. The climate isn't too extreme, even in the winter."

"But it's not home." Even if it was pretty here, Mount Juliet would always and forever be my home.

"Now that's a true statement" He pulled me into his arms. "And soon, after all this is over, we'll return to lead both the Murphy and Rogers packs."

"That sounds so far-fetched." However, that was the only way we could return.

"Nope. For both witches and shifters to believe it, it has to be true, and we're going to win." He lowered his head, and his lips touched mine.

I responded to his kiss, desperate for more. I had to believe he was right, or what was the point?

Even though I wanted to focus only on us, I pulled back. "Why do you think the wolves are getting antsy?"

"I'm sure it has to do with the girl we're looking for." Aidan frowned. "It seems like wherever we go, the girls are in some sort of trouble."

"Technically, Ivory wasn't." She'd been with a coven that was hiding her.

"Those wolves were determined to get her." His arms squeezed my waist. "Now they know about us, and I guarantee the various Hallowed Guild packs are touching base and preparing for something."

"I'm hoping we don't have to go to war." I wasn't sure we'd survive it. "We just need to get the girls back to Columbus before they find us." Things were becoming serious and fast.

"You're right, but tonight, we need to rest and go with clear heads tomorrow to hunt her." He cupped my face.

I heard the other doors shut in succession; everyone was in their rooms, settling in for the night.

He linked with me. *Can we not worry about it all and just focus on each other?* His golden eyes glowed, alerting me that his wolf was taking partial control.

My body warmed at the promise of his words. *Maybe.* I pretended to put up a fight, even though I had no plans on following through.

Well, then let me be more persuasive. He lowered his mouth and brushed his tongue against my lips.

I opened my mouth, enjoying his minty taste. I doubted I'd ever get tired of it.

Desperate need coursed through me as the buzzing of

our bond made my head dizzy. I reached down, grabbed the hem of his shirt, and yanked it over his head.

He must have been feeling the same way as me, because he removed my shirt and pulled me against his naked chest.

The feel of his skin against mine warmed me even more.

His fingers worked on the clasp of my bra, and soon, he peeled it from my body. His calloused hands cupped my breast as I walked backward to the bed. My hands went to the buttons of his jeans and undid them. Then I pushed his jeans and boxers down.

Dammit, hold on. He pulled away, chuckling as he kicked off his shoes and his clothing to the ground.

My eyes took in every inch of his hard, gorgeous body.

He pushed me to the bed, yanked my shoes off, and tossed them across the room. In the next second, his lips were on my stomach and kissing lower as he worked on my pants. His teeth gently scraped against my skin, and a moan escaped me.

A low growl vibrated through him. *These are in the way.* He slid my panties and pants off, and then his lips crashed against mine.

Needing him desperately, I reached down and touched him.

Dear God. He moaned in my head.

His hands slipped down and began rubbing, causing friction in the right spot. It didn't take long before I was coming too damn close.

I pushed him off me and turned over on the bed so I was on my hands and knees. I wanted us to do something different from the other times.

Are you sure? He climbed on the bed and positioned himself right against my ass.

Yes, please.

He thrust inside me, hitting deeper than ever before. I rocked back against him as we increased our pace. He wrapped his fingers around my waist as he slammed into me time and time again.

Our breathing grew rapid as he pounded into me. I was so close to the edge that when he raked his teeth against the back of my neck, my body contracted and waves of pleasure exploded inside me. I orgasmed harder than ever before.

A guttural groan came from him as he finished, and we plopped down on the bed and rolled onto our backs, trying to calm our racing hearts.

The next morning, we all met up in the dining room and found eggs, bacon, toast, and hash browns on the table. We all filled our plates and went to the back, looking out toward the mountains, and pushed three black wire tables together. The brown chairs were outdoor ones, so not super comfortable, but the view made up for it.

"Now that we've checked out, what's our plan?" Remus took a bite of his eggs and chewed.

"We go hiking and wait for a tug." That's all I had. If it was anything like the other two times, our connection should lead us to her.

"What if there isn't one?" Ivory asked.

"Then, we'll regroup, but my gut says it'll happen." We had counted on our magic guiding us so far, and I had no other way of finding her.

"The locator spell got us here." Amethyst smiled and took a sip of her orange juice. "Magic always has a way of helping out when needed."

The table went silent as we ate and enjoyed being

outside and part of nature. The mountains rolled as far as we could see, and I felt at peace just staring at them.

A loud howl came from no more than ten miles away. It was full of angst and pain.

Of course, that's when the tugging started. I jumped to my feet and looked at the others. "We have to go."

CHAPTER EIGHTEEN

"Wait ..." Aidan said as he grabbed my hand, holding me still. "We need to think this through and be cautious. There's no telling what's going on."

"Maybe, but I feel the tug too." Gabby stood as well and nodded at me. "Our girl is either hurt or around a person who is. She might need our help."

"I'm not saying we don't go." Aidan raised his other hand. "I'm just saying we have to be careful. We can't rush out there and risk becoming outnumbered. For all we know, The Hallowed Guild is already here."

Shit, I hadn't even thought that far ahead. "You're right." I hated that, and it proved I needed to stop and listen to my mate even if it was the last thing I wanted to do.

"Is everything okay out here?" The hostess stepped outside and stared at our group. Her eyes flicked back behind her. "Some people in here are concerned about what's going on."

"Yeah, everything is fine." Amethyst leaned back in her seat, pretending to be relaxed.

"Okay, you all may want to come in ..." She trailed off as if searching for the right word. "A wolf sounds close by."

Maybe a B&B wasn't the best idea. I hadn't considered how much closer we would be in proximity to the humans and how they could complain easily to the owner.

We needed cheap, and we got a night's rest. Aidan stood and turned to the lady. "We were finishing up and about to go on a hike."

"Well, be careful." The lady looked at us like we were crazy as she stepped back into the house and shut the door.

"Let's go." Ivory pushed her chair under the table. "If she's in trouble, we need to make a plan."

"Let's take our plates in and go," Beth said as she collected her dirty dishes.

We all hurried, and soon, we were heading down the concrete path to the beginning of the woods.

"Do you think we should shift?" Ivory rubbed her hands together.

"Not at first. Since we aren't a pack, we can't communicate in our wolf forms." I wondered if, once we fulfilled the prophecy, there would be an exception to the rule between me and the girls since we had a witchy connection.

"Maybe a few of us should turn." Logan pointed at himself, Remus, and Aidan. "We can use the mate bond to connect with you."

"Wait ..." I looked at Gabby as the off scent finally made sense. "You guys bonded?" Now that he'd said that, I noticed the faint scar of teeth marks on her neck. "Why didn't you tell us?"

"Because it was between him and me." Gabby lifted her chin, ready to argue.

She'd been less confrontational but still wasn't letting

me in. I was glad that this might allow her to feel more secure with herself.

"I think that's a good idea." Ivory scanned our surroundings.

"Then, let's go shift." Aidan kissed my cheek. "We'll run over to the section of woods and change. That way we can find our clothes easily when we get back."

"Okay, hurry." It felt like the more seconds that passed by, the more injured the girl could get.

The three of them took off as we continued our trek down to where the concrete turned into earth.

"Won't the other wolves be able to smell them better if they shift?" Samuel looked at me.

"Yeah, but we're stronger in wolf form." I understood their hesitancy. We'd always wanted to fly under the radar, but this situation already seemed riskier than the prior two marked girls.

"Hey, I'm down with that." Coral patted her chest. "I'm not out to be a shero."

"Shero?" Beth bobbed her head, letting her blue hair fall over her shoulder.

"Hell, yeah. Shero." Coral lifted her chin. "Hero is totally sexist."

"I like it." Gabby grinned.

The guys ran to the wood's edge, entering the woods enough to fall into the shadows. The last thing we needed was for a human to see three wolves running around after what the lady had told us last night.

Our group of seven joined them, and we all took off down a well-worn trail.

"We need to venture off the common path." Shifters wouldn't be hanging around the more heavily populated areas.

Aidan linked with me as he trotted westward. *I think the howl came from this direction.*

The tug was pulling me that way too, so it made sense. "We need to go this way," I informed the others as we all followed behind him.

Remus stayed to the right of our group, next to Ivory, while Logan stayed to the left, near Gabby. I took the lead with Beth right behind me, and the witches in the rear. Right now, there wasn't a threat, but that could change in a second.

We moved at a good clip, and two miles into the woods, we picked up the musky scent of at least five wolves.

I turned around and placed my finger to my lips. The witches couldn't smell it, so I needed to signal them to be quiet.

Amethyst stood in the middle, and her eyes caught mine. She nodded as she touched one hand to Coral's shoulder and the other to Samuel's, alerting them to me.

The metallic scent of blood hung in the air, which meant someone was injured.

That can't be a good sign. Aidan trotted over to some low branches.

My eyes followed him, and I almost gagged when I saw trickles of blood along the trees and ground. *Oh my God.*

Calm down. Maybe she isn't the one who's injured. Aidan tried to be comforting, but his concern pulsed off him. He was worried as well.

Even though I wanted to panic, I pushed it back. If I let my fear take over, I could put us in danger. If one of us died, it was all over. Then some other poor girls in the future would be burdened with the curse.

The trees became denser, and our group had to form a

straight line. Remus took the center, between Ivory and Beth. Logan took charge of the back.

The thick line of blood that painted the ground thinned. The injured wolf's healing abilities had kicked in, which was a blessing. That meant the injury hadn't been fatal.

Aidan followed the scent, and I didn't stop him. He was heading in the direction I wanted to go.

With each step, the tug grew stronger. With each girl, the connection amplified. It was like two magnets pulling together.

I heard faint voices, which meant we were getting close to whoever we were tracking. I couldn't make out the words yet, but I'd be able to in a few minutes.

Our group wasn't walking fast. We were being slow and methodical. Under different circumstances, this would have been a lovely place to run wild and free. The temperature was in the low forties, and nature was alive and all around. The trees were lush and so thick it blocked out the sun. If it hadn't been for the cry, I never would have thought something was amiss.

"She really thought she could escape?" A deep, vicious voice asked.

"We'll have to put that stupid bitch in her place." Another man chuckled with delight. "I mean, what better way to keep them all in line?"

Is this The Hallowed Guild? They apparently treated their women like they weren't important.

I don't think so. Aidan kept his steady pace. *I haven't heard of a branch here, but that doesn't mean things haven't changed. Dad keeps close watch on the Guild packs.*

Oh, really? Now that he said it, it made sense that he would.

Remember our pack is directly descended from the original alpha? Aidan used to sound like he was in turmoil whenever he spoke about his family, but now it was as if he'd accepted that they were our enemies.

But I didn't even consider that he'd be keeping track of them. I needed to be thinking more strategically.

He makes his rounds to all Guild packs every couple of years. I only know of five packs, and this isn't one.

Well, at least, we had that going for us.

"I still can't believe that girl ran off," the deeper-voiced man spoke again. "Maybe they need a reminder that they're our property."

The worst type of people were the ones who got off on hurting others. It was a damn shame that some packs were led by such heartless alphas.

We were inching up on the pack's grounds, and luckily, the wolves seemed none the wiser. Old wooden houses had seen better days. The roofs were sagging, and the walls were rotted.

Let's go this way. Aidan led us away from the men's voices.

That's where I'm being pulled anyway. Luckily, those two idiots weren't with her.

We stuck to the trees as we quickly walked around the clearing where they'd made their home. It wasn't large, but at least sixty houses were spread out. They were small with only a couple of rooms if that.

The strong scent of blood stopped me in my tracks. The coppery smell revolted inside my stomach.

"Dear God, what happened?" a young woman asked from only a few feet away.

Aidan moved so we could all pile under some brush next to a large tree. The seven of us got down on our knees and huddled out of view next to the men still in their wolf form.

The girl who must have spoken rushed by two poorly built houses and ran over to the tree line. She dropped to her knees next to someone curled up in a ball on the ground.

The girl leaned over the body, her dark hair cascading down her shoulders. "What did you do?" she asked as she reached out her dark olive hand toward the injured person.

The pull was so damn strong that there was no denying it. One of those girls was a chosen one.

"I just wanted to leave." The other girl moved, and her dark brown hair spilled across the green grass. "Mom died last night, which means ..." The girl groaned as she sat upright and clutched her side.

"You don't have any protection." The darker-haired girl huffed. "Why didn't you tell me?"

"Because I took off this morning." The girl moved her hand, revealing her blood-soaked shirt. "It didn't do much good."

"You made things so much worse, Ada." The darker girl rubbed her arms. "They'll make an example out of you, which is bad. We're the last two women who haven't been mated off."

"Honor, you know what our fates will be if we stay here. You'll be forced to mate with that sicko alpha and me his beta." The girl turned slightly before she stopped and winced. "We need something more to go on."

The tug was so overwhelmingly hard I couldn't handle it anymore. *I'm going to talk to her.*

What? No. He shook his wolf head hard several times.

Before I could stand, footsteps pounded in their direction.

"Shit, here they come." Honor stood in front of the girl, blocking her.

"You'd better leave before …" Ada trailed off.

"Now, why am I not surprised to find Honor here?" The one with the cruel voice stepped into view. He was about my height, which I hadn't expected, but he was large. He had long, greasy, mousy-brown hair pulled back into a man bun. He crossed his arms over his mammoth chest as his icy green gaze focused on her.

"It's for the best." Another guy came into view. He was the same height but smaller, with oily dark hair. His forehead shone as if you could skate on it, and his dead eyes locked on Ada, who could only partially be seen behind Honor. "We don't have to find her."

"She's already hurt." Honor cleared her throat. "Haven't you done enough?" She stared the bigger guy down.

"Apparently not since you're acting so defiant." The alpha flashed across the space between them and grabbed Honor by the throat. "You see, there's a big problem. You and Ada think you're more than you are." He squeezed her throat, and she coughed. "We need to teach you both your place." He let go, and the girl fell to her knees.

Everything inside me told me to go and help them.

Aidan connected with me, barely in the nick of time. *If you go, the whole pack will descend. We won't make it out alive.*

He was right, but dammit, what kind of person sat back and watched this?

As soon as Honor moved to stand, the alpha punched her right in the side.

She cried out and collapsed to the ground.

Gabby moved to get on her feet, but Logan nabbed her hand with his mouth, keeping her still.

"Stop it," Ada yelled from the ground. As she tried to stand, the beta leaned over her and dug his fingers right into her wound. Blood sprouted on her clothes, and she crumbled back onto the ground.

"You don't get to tell us what to do," the sicko said as he smiled, watching tears pour down Ada's face as she shivered in pain.

"You know what? Enough is enough." The alpha turned to his friend. "We mate with them tonight. I'm done with their ways."

What kind of monsters were they? I'd never seen such vile creatures before.

"Sounds like a plan." The guy chuckled and let go of the girl. "I guess we shouldn't hurt them too bad. That's what tonight is for."

"Enjoy your last little bit of freedom. Tonight, we'll own you soul and all." The alpha laughed as he turned and walked away. "Oh, and if you run, we'll find you."

Hell, no. That wouldn't happen. Those girls were leaving with us.

CHAPTER NINETEEN

We have to talk to them. Our scent was already too close for comfort. I couldn't waltz over there and broadcast our presence.

Emma ... Aidan's warning was clear in my head.

I watched the two retreating figures. They swaggered away from the girls, proud of what they'd done. They expected the girls to bend to their will. The one girl was too hurt to make a run for it without help from our witches.

I needed to find something ... anything to get their attention. My eyes located a small branch. It wouldn't make a ton of noise to alert the whole damn pack, but I thought it should be enough to get the girls' attention.

We had to get them out of here, I didn't figure it should be an issue since they were both desperate to leave.

Our group had loaded our luggage into the car in case of a situation like this. We never knew what we were walking into and needed to be prepared to leave at a second's notice.

I grabbed the branch and turned to the rest of our group. I motioned to the stick and toward them, trying to communicate without words.

Thankfully, we were on the same page. I placed my finger to my lips, making sure the witches knew to stay quiet. I knew the wolves did. They understood how wolf hearing worked, but the witches didn't.

Coral nodded, letting me know at least she understood. She was the loudmouth of the three with Samuel as a close second.

I'm going to throw this at them, so be ready in case the two men come back. With the ten of us, we could take down the alpha and beta as long as they didn't call for pack help.

I took a deep breath to calm my heart and clear my thoughts. I had to get the branch close enough to them so they could find me. I stood and lopped it toward them. It landed three feet away from them.

Honor tensed and turned in my direction. Her eyes widened when they found me. She opened her mouth to say something, but I put my finger to my lips. I hadn't even considered they'd be too shocked or scared to stay quiet.

"What the hell was that?" Ada clutched her side, her face lined with pain as she tried to turn.

"Nothing." Honor's eyes stayed on me as she nodded in my direction.

Ada looked at me, and her mouth dropped.

Well, at least they weren't hollering for help. I waved them over. I hated to make Ada walk, but we had no choice.

"Here." Honor kneeled and grabbed her best friend's shoulders. "On the count of three. One ... two ... three." She helped Ada to her feet.

"Dear God." Ada groaned through clenched teeth. Tears sprang in her eyes, and she blinked them away. "Damn, that hurt." She glanced down at the blood pooling at the site.

"We'll need to clean it and cover it up." Honor's voice was even, as if nothing was out of the ordinary.

"That sounds painful." Ada frowned as they made their way toward me with slow, steady steps. Within seconds, they'd walked all the way into the thicker trees and right to me.

"Who are you?" Honor's voice was so low that the witches probably hadn't heard her. "Are you here to hurt us? There are so many of you."

For her not to be alarmed proved our connection was working on her too. A sane wolf wouldn't have come over like she had. To prevent having to explain too much, I turned around and moved my hair to the side, showing my mark.

Ada's breath caught as she looked. "Holy shit. That's similar to yours."

So Honor was the one we were here for. I pointed at Gabby and Ivory and motioned for them to stand. I wanted Honor to see that there were three people like her.

They followed my lead without question and rose. They showed their marks that were more like hers.

"It's like your marks go in order," Ada said a little too loud for comfort.

"We're here to take you with us." I met Honor's eyes. "I can explain what it all means once we're out of here." My voice was so low the breeze could have blown the words away.

Honor's eyes filled with hope. "I'm not going without her."

Aidan, I think ...

Of course, we're taking her. Aidan nuzzled my hand with his snout. *We can't leave her behind to be mated with that asshole.*

I loved that man so much. "There was no question."

"Really?" Ada sounded like her breath had been knocked out of her.

I nodded. "But we need to get going." I gestured for the others to get up.

"We need to move fast, but she's injured." Hysteria infiltrated Honor's voice.

Amethyst stepped toward us and said, keeping her voice low, "I can help." She held out her hands. "May I?"

Ada stepped toward her. "Please." Her eyes were desperate.

Amethyst touched the girl's injury and closed her eyes. The surrounding air became charged as she pulled magic from nature. The thrumming in my skin that used to be foreign now felt natural. It didn't make my blood crawl anymore because I was more attuned to it. I could even feel the magic coming from the ground and coursing through my feet and legs.

I watched in awe as the blood stopped, and Ada took smoother breaths.

"The injury isn't completely healed, but you'll be able to move easier." Amethyst bent down and rubbed the excess blood from her hand on the ground.

"I think I can handle the pain now." Ada's light brown eyes sparkled.

"Then, we need to go. Even if she's not as injured, we can't move as fast," Beth whispered. "Right now, they are celebrating beating the shit out of Ada and forcing Honor and her hand into being mated. We need to get as much distance between us as possible while we have the advantage."

"Okay. Let's get up and moving," Ivory said, not needing any additional encouragement.

We all moved back into the trees to stay out of sight, and Remus took the lead with Ivory, the witches, Ada, and Honor following behind. Then, Gabby and Logan were in the middle with Beth, me, and Aidan right behind.

Our group hurried back around the pack's home. The faster we got out of this area, the less risk involved. At some point, they would notice the girls were gone.

We have thirty minutes tops. Aidan linked with me as he scanned the area, waiting for something to pop out.

I was hoping for an hour or so. Granted, I wasn't sure what the girls' responsibilities were in the pack.

Either another woman will notice their absence, or Dumb and Dumber will come back to taunt them some more. Contempt rang in Aidan's mind. *And for us to be near humans won't deter those jackasses from attacking. So we need to be gone before they realize we were ever here.*

But that's against the law. We couldn't alert the humans to us.

Jackasses like them can't be rationalized with. They think of the girls as their property and will do whatever it takes to get them back.

Of course, they did. I hated that Ada and Honor had grown up being treated as objects. I imagined that couldn't be emotionally healthy. *At least, they wanted to go.* Some people caught in abusive cycles were scared to leave what they knew.

She was made to be strong. Aidan ran forward and butted his head against my leg. *And it looks like she's her friend's strength too. I'm sure they didn't come out unscathed, but they'll survive.*

I'd make sure they did.

Our group was in sync and moving seamlessly. I could

tell that Ada was struggling. She was holding on to her side, but she didn't let the injury slow her down.

Once we were several miles away from the pack, I breathed a sigh of relief.

But it was way too soon.

"Shit." Honor stopped in her tracks and looked back. "They know we're gone."

Ada huffed, "They're coming. They've picked up our scent."

"We need to hurry!" Gabby hollered at Remus.

Honor's dark eyes filled with worry. "Can you go faster?"

"Hell, yeah. As long as we get away from them, I can manage it." Ada nodded.

"Then we're going." Ivory took off after Remus, moving twice as fast.

It wasn't nearly as fast as we could go, but with Ada and the witches, it was the fastest we could make it.

Remus, Logan, and I need to turn around and meet them head-on. Aidan ran steadily behind me. *It's the only way we can hold them off and you can drive the Suburbans down the mountain. We can meet you at the base so we don't take the enemy wolves to the bed-and-breakfast. We need to protect the humans staying there.*

This was what made Aidan so different from his pack and others. He cared about not only his own kind but the humans too. *I want to go with you.*

The girls need you. His words were full of conviction. *You're the glue holding all this together. Gabby is here because of you. If you leave or worse, there's no telling what might happen.*

Fine. I didn't like it, but he was right. We couldn't take the wolves back to the house. The wolves would harm as many as necessary to get Ada and Honor back. *But if anything goes south, you tell me immediately.*

I promise. His commitment to the words poured through our bond.

Now, it was time to piss Gabby and Ivory off. "Hey, Aidan wants him and the ..." Maybe if I didn't say their names, it wouldn't elicit such a strong reaction. "... other two wolves to double back and head them off so we can get to the vehicles and protect the humans."

"What?" Gabby spun around, and Beth almost ran into her. "Hell, no."

This was what I'd expected, especially from her. "Look, we all need to stay together, and they're already in wolf form. Aidan promised to let me know if they need backup. If they do, we'll hurry back to them right then and there."

She and Logan must have been mind-linking because she got quiet for a moment before blowing out a breath. "Of course, you'd gang up on me. Fine, but if he gets severely injured, it's on both of you." Gabby looked at me and then Logan. "And I won't be nice."

She wouldn't. She'd been ornery ever since the night everything had come out. "I'd expect no less."

"Remus wants to, so I can't stand in his way." Ivory nodded. "Even if I'm not thrilled about it."

Her relationship with Remus was one of the strongest I'd ever seen. They respected each other and didn't push each other around. Those were relationship goals I hoped Aidan and I could achieve one day. Granted, we were getting better at it already.

With each of our blessings, the wolves separated from the group and ran back toward the pack.

"We still need to hurry. The longer they have to fight, the bigger the chance that our mates could be injured." I knew all of them were strong alpha wolves, but that didn't mean they were indestructible.

That's all I needed to say to get Ivory rushing forward again.

Our group took off at a good pace once more. We were only about five miles from the bed-and-breakfast.

I hated that Aidan had headed back to confront the wolves. That group appeared particularly vicious and uncaring, so they'd do any type of fighting necessary to win. *They'll probably fight dirty.*

There's no doubt in my mind. Aidan linked back with me immediately. *We're getting close, but don't worry. The three of us know what we're doing. Just get down the mountain so we can meet you.* He unlinked with me.

I wanted to connect with him again, but if they were fighting, I didn't want to distract him.

Only thirty minutes passed, but it felt like a lifetime. Soon, we were out of the woods and back to where the concrete sidewalk would take us to the house.

"Hold on a second." I rushed to the area the guys had changed and grabbed their clothes. I tried not to focus on carrying Remus's and Logan's underwear. Aidan's didn't bother me, of course.

When I ran from the woods, Beth snapped her fingers and said, "Good call."

We'd all packed light, so every outfit was precious. We had to slow our pace back up to the house. We couldn't walk faster than what was normal for a human.

As we walked into the house, a couple was still at the breakfast table, and their eyes immediately went to Ada's shirt.

"Was she stabbed?" The girl jumped to her feet and stumbled away.

Crap, I hadn't even considered that.

"What's going on here?" The owner entered the room, and her eyes almost bugged out of her head when she took Ada in. "What the hell ... I thought you all had already left after checking out"

We didn't have time for this. "We're leaving here now."

"Thank God." She waved us to the door. "You've made so many people uncomfortable, and this is the icing on the cake." She pointed to Ada.

It was nice to know the bitch was more worried about her guests than an injured girl. But this made things easier and faster. "Okay then."

Our group raced out the front door, and we divided up in the cars. This time, Ivory went with the witches and Beth whereas Ada and Honor joined me.

"This is a sweet ride." Ada sighed as she settled in. "I'll try not to get blood on the seats."

"Don't worry about it. Just get situated." I turned the key in the ignition, pulled out from the house, and headed down the mountain.

Emma. Aidan linked with me. *We are heading to the east toward the base of the mountain. You need to get there fast. I'm not sure how much longer we can keep the upper hand. They've called in backup.*

Those words sent terror coursing through my body.

CHAPTER TWENTY

Aidan

Like I figured, the two jackasses were overconfident and came alone. My dad was the same way. They believed they were more powerful and stronger than they were. Growing up, I used to admire that, thinking that because of his confidence, he must have been the most alpha in the United States—possibly the world.

But it wasn't that. It was because he was a narcissist and didn't care about anyone, not even his sons. He'd raised us to be the same way—proud when we hurt others. We were his legacy, and the more we acted like him, the stronger and more ruthless he appeared.

Remus, Logan, and I formed a circle, with our butts almost touching. We were protecting each other's backs. I could see Remus's brown fur on my right and Logan's almost white fur on my left.

The two douchebags were in their wolf forms as well. It was easy to distinguish the two despite their slight differences in color. The alpha was huge, which was making fighting them more difficult.

I hated linking with Emma and scaring her. But the douchebags were strong, and I'd needed to get a sense of where they were. We'd been fighting them and holding them off, but it was taking all three of us against the two. Backup would be here any second, and when they were, we'd be screwed.

We needed to take them down and get to the vehicles. Even though the three of us couldn't communicate, I was pretty damn sure we were on the same page.

Remus launched at the beta, leaving me and Logan to take down the alpha. We were trying to switch it up so they weren't sure which one of us would attack who.

I glanced at Logan, and he nodded. We hunkered to the ground while the large alpha ran toward us.

We needed to catch him off guard. I dug my paws into the ground and charged right at the alpha. He anticipated a fight, and when he was two feet from me, he stood on his hind legs, ready for me to do the same. Instead, I dropped to the ground, and the asshole stumbled over me and fell to the ground.

Logan must have read my mind because, as soon as the douchebag fell, he was on top of him, digging his teeth right into the guy's throat.

Okay ... we weren't communicating clearly after all. The point had been to weaken them so we could get away, not kill them.

A second passed before I forced the shock away. I needed to save this guy. We didn't need both The Hallowed Guild and another psycho pack hunting us.

Before I could reach him, Logan yanked his head to the side, ripping the guy's throat out.

No ... no! This couldn't be happening.

The beta must have felt his alpha die because he stumbled back from Remus and ran over to his packmate.

Logan bared his teeth at the beta, blood dripping from his mouth and onto the ground.

No, we couldn't do that. If I thought taking these two assholes out would make a difference, I wouldn't pause, but other men would eagerly take their places. Their pack had been raised to behave like this, and it would take something out of the ordinary to break the cycle.

Emma, I need you to get Gabby to tell Logan to come there now. I hated to put her in the middle, but Gabby was the only one who could make him leave. *Otherwise, he's going to kill again.*

Again? Horror filled our bond, her words almost breathless. *What do you mean "again"?*

Babe, I'll tell you everything, but right now, I need Gabby to link with him. I didn't mean to be short with her, but she was my only hope. I didn't have time to keep repeating myself.

Okay.

Our connection went completely silent, and I watched Logan closely. At the first sign of him attacking the beta, I would intervene.

Right now, we needed to be searching for the next girl, not killing.

Logan stilled, which gave me hope that Gabby was working her magic.

She's talking to him. Emma connected with me. *Honor just informed us that she lost her link with her alpha. Did Logan have anything to do with that?*

He killed the alpha. I couldn't stop it. I felt so damn responsible. *We can't communicate, and Logan went dark.*

It wasn't your fault, Emma said softly.

Maybe. I couldn't help but feel guilty. Emma was the girls' leader, which meant I should be the men's. This was all on me.

Logan's white eyes flashed to mine, and he nodded.

He'd come back down from whatever had possessed him and not a moment too soon. I jerked my head toward where we needed to go, and Remus took off.

I watched Logan's freaky eyes glance back to the beta. The beta was howling in pain at the loss of their leader.

He was calling the others.

Without giving another damn, I turned and followed Remus for a few steps, hoping that would wake up Logan. We needed to get back to the girls we loved.

After a few strides, I spun around to see what Logan would do.

The white wolf flicked his head back to me and then the beta. After a second, he huffed and turned to follow me.

I pushed my legs hard to catch up with Remus. The trees flew past us as we raced to safety.

I kept listening behind me, ensuring Logan stayed behind us. I didn't need him turning around and trying to finish the job.

Remus slowed, waiting for us.

It made me like him more. He wouldn't abandon us. It wasn't something I'd expect Logan to do.

As we ran, I surveyed the surrounding trees. We were getting closer to the base of the mountain, but I wasn't relieved yet. I was sure the pack was hunting us down.

After what felt like hours but was only minutes, we were almost at the cars. *Emma, we should be there in ten minutes.*

Okay, great. Emma sounded relieved. *We are here and waiting on you. I'll tell the others to be prepared.*

Sounds great. I needed to be with her again.

The trees thinned around us, giving us our first hint that civilization was close. My heart had begun to slow its rapid pace when several pain-stricken howls came from behind us and fairly close by. The wolves were on the hunt.

Emma connected with me again. *Please tell me you're still okay.*

There was no question. She'd heard the howls too. *Yes. They're after us, though. We should be fine. Just be ready.*

I swear, each place we go, it gets crazier and crazier.

She wasn't wrong. After a few minutes, the two Suburbans came into view. They were right at the edge of the road, by the cliff.

Both vehicles' back doors were open.

That had me running even faster.

Paws pounded behind us. The pack drew closer. They knew the woods and could navigate them quicker and more efficiently.

The three of us sprinted harder. Remus jumped in Samuel's vehicle with Ivory, while Logan jumped in then squeezed into the backseat with Gabby.

Emma pushed open the passenger side door for me. She sat straight in the driver's seat, and I leaped into the vehicle.

"I've got it." Honor slammed the door shut for me right as a few wolves broke through the tree line and came toward us.

Samuel peeled out with Emma following right behind, driving as fast as possible to the city.

I lay down on the front passenger seat, facing Emma. I was finally home again.

Emma

IT SCARED the living hell out of me to watch those three run to us with fear in their eyes. They were being hunted like prey, which pissed me off. This had been the theme this past month since I'd learned what I was.

We followed the main roads into the city, making sure not to take side roads where we'd have to slow down. My eyes kept going to the rearview mirror, but I hadn't seen the wolves chasing after us for the last five miles.

Samuel got on the interstate and headed south. We followed, racing to put some distance between us and the wolves. The guys needed to shift back into human form so we could figure out our next stop.

"What's our plan?" Honor asked from the passenger side, middle row seat.

Crap, I hadn't really told her anything. "We'll pull over soon to let the guys shift and perform the spell that'll tell us where the last girl is."

"You're still looking for one more?" Ada sounded shocked, but I couldn't be sure since she was sitting right behind me.

"Yes, there are five of us in total." At least, I wasn't as clueless anymore.

"But you don't know where she is?" Honor shook her head as if she couldn't believe what she'd just heard.

I filled them in on everything, and the moment I finished, Samuel pulled off on a low-populated exit and stopped on the side of the road.

He got out of the car, and so did everyone else except Remus.

Beth hurried over, and I rolled my window down.

"Let's find out where we're heading while they get back in normal form." Beth winked at Aidan and chuckled. "He looks miserable."

"Their clothes are in the trunk." I opened the door, got out, and headed to the back. I turned around to find Beth not there with me. "Hey, get your ass back here."

"What? Why?" Beth approached, her brows furrowed.

"Because you get to bring Remus his clothes." I grabbed his clothes and handed them to her.

"Wait ... are those his underwear?" Beth's face creased.

"Hey, I had to carry them from the woods to the vehicle." She wasn't getting any sympathy from me. "Think of this as your punishment."

"For what?" She took the clothes and held them as far from her body as she could.

"I don't know, but I'm sure you're due something." I forced a smile on my face.

"Well played," she grumbled as she walked to the other vehicle. "But you've just declared war."

That actually concerned me. "Gabby, grab your man's clothes, and I'll take Aidan his." I carried Aidan's clothes to the front and put them on the center console. "I'll get the witches to perform the spell in front of their car so you can shift in peace."

The rest of our group climbed out, and we headed to the lead Suburban.

Amethyst stepped out of the car and held up the map. "We're ready."

Our remaining group of nine laid the map on the dirt ground. The tree line was to the right, but we were at least twenty miles from Ojai, so there was no way the wolves could find us with our path gone cold.

Amethyst spread it out even on the ground, and Samuel and Coral squatted on either side, holding it open for me.

"Now, let's begin." Amethyst nodded at me.

We went in the order of the points on the star. Since I'd started the journey, I was up first. It wasn't long before I, Gabby, and Ivory had dripped our blood on the map.

"Now Honor, you do the same," Coral said as she nodded to the newest member of the club.

"The blood literally moved across the map." Honor blinked several times as if she thought she was seeing things.

"Yup, and their blood directed us to where we are since you're with us." Samuel glanced at her hand. "When you add yours to the map, we'll know where the next girl is."

"That's freaky, but damn." Ada grinned. "Go for it. I want to see."

Honor bit her finger. Her hands shook as she held it out, and she licked her bottom lip. When she turned her hand over, the blood mixed with ours, and the blob began to move once more.

We watched it head southeast and land on Austin, Texas.

Now, we'd wait to see what we'd find once we got there.

CHAPTER TWENTY-ONE

Aidan

I'd been steaming the whole ride. I tried to keep my mouth shut since everyone's adrenaline was crashing after the fight, but the more I thought about Logan's actions, the madder I got.

Samuel pulled into a Holiday Inn parking lot where we planned on staying tonight. I got out of the car, slammed the door, and headed to the trunk to get my and Emma's things.

Logan joined me and grabbed his bag. "What the hell is your problem?"

"You." It was that simple.

"I saved our asses back there." Logan huffed.

"What's going on?" Emma walked over to us while Gabby appeared on the other side.

"This moron thinks he saved us by killing the alpha." He was delusional.

"I did, and if I'd taken the beta down too, we'd be even safer." Logan lifted his chin in defiance.

"Aidan's right. You've guaranteed that another pack will

be hunting us." Remus stood next to me. "So, now we have two enemies instead of one."

"Don't be upset because he did something neither one of you could do." Gabby sneered. "I only asked him to stop because I know Emma would have left his ass behind."

"You better stop right there." Emma's gray eyes glowed, and she looked damn beautiful. "Whether you like it or not, you're part of this, which means our decisions are made as a team. Remus was on Aidan's side, so Logan should've stood down. I may need you, but you need us more. The Hallowed Guild is searching for us, and we have a coven that we can stay with that has offered us protection and to ride this out if need be. So get on board before we have to cut our liabilities." She stepped toward them, her wolf surging more.

Gabby tried to challenge her, but before long, she averted her eyes. That's when she looked at Logan.

"I won't make you submit to me as your alpha, but you better respect Aidan and me."

Logan barely nodded.

That's when I knew, with Emma as our leader, we might survive this.

Emma

THREE DAYS LATER, we rolled into Austin, Texas. I wasn't sure what I'd expected, but the town was gorgeous. I could even see myself living here, which was saying something.

It was ten in the morning. I'd considered stopping to get a hotel room, but with the way things were going, if we found the girl, we'd need to leave town as fast as possible.

My phone rang, and I pulled it from my pocket. Beth's name flashed on the caller ID. I swiped ANSWER and held it to my ear. "Hello?"

"Hey, Amethyst looked at the map again," Beth said. I heard Coral say something from the front seat, and Beth paused.

"Oh, bite me," Samuel huffed in response.

"Everything okay?" Everyone's nerves were shot, and the tension was almost palpable. Being on the run and constantly in danger was wearing on us.

"Yeah, Coral is accusing Samuel of farting." Beth sighed. "It smells like manure in here."

"Just admit it." Coral's voice rose. "We need to roll down the windows."

"You smelled it, you dealt it," Samuel called out as the sound of windows lowering and wind blowing into the car filled my ears.

"Will you two quit," Beth growled. "Coral, we all know it was you, so stop messing around."

"How so?" Coral said indignantly.

Beth gagged. "Because we're wolves and can smell the origin."

Oh my God. I was so glad I wasn't in the same car. I should've known that Beth, Coral, and Samuel might scare Ivory and Remus away.

"Oh, so what are you going to do? Sniff my ass to confirm?" The embarrassment was clear in Coral's voice.

"No, I'm not an animal—wait, I am, but not a dog. I won't be doing that anytime soon," Beth replied.

"It's okay, we all do it," Ivory said sweetly.

"Beth, can you focus on your conversation with Emma?" Annoyance filled Amethyst's usually warm voice.

"Oh, yeah." Beth waved a hand in front of her nose. "Sorry, it smells like shit in here ... literally."

"They couldn't be normal," Aidan muttered loud enough for only me to hear.

A laugh broke free before I could contain it. "Yeah, I gathered that. What's up?"

"We're going to let you lead in case you feel something." Beth cleared her throat. "Amethyst looked, and she's slightly north of Austin. With three of you in your car, you may notice the tug before we do."

"Okay, that makes sense." I turned to Aidan. "Get in front of Samuel. They want us to lead."

"Got it." Aidan nodded.

"Oh, and you three try not to kill each other." Whatever frustrations they had, they needed to get it out before we started hunting for our girl.

"There are six of us in the car," Beth scoffed.

"Your point?" I smiled, even though she couldn't see it. "I'm not worried about Amethyst, Ivory, or Remus."

"You've got me there." Beth chuckled. "Okay, I'm sure we'll talk soon. We'll follow your lead from here on out."

I ended the call and shook my head.

"Everything okay?" Honor leaned over the center console so I could see her.

"Yeah, just everyone's nerves are on edge." I looked over my shoulder. "How's everyone back there?"

"Fine, if Gabby and Logan could stop sucking face," Ada growled.

Okay, maybe we were not better off than the other vehicle. I hadn't been willing to turn around too often for that same reason.

"Hey, don't be jealous." Gabby grinned. "I'm sure you'll find someone."

"I'm not jealous." Ada wrinkled her nose. "I don't want a man. It's the furthest thing from my mind after that hell we left behind."

Couldn't blame her there. "The three of us"—I pointed at Gabby, Honor, and myself—"need to focus. As soon as we feel a tug, we need to alert Aidan."

"So ... how does this work?" Honor bit her bottom lip. "I mean, I'm not sure what to expect."

"It's what she said ... a tug." Gabby arched an eyebrow as if that explained it.

Honor's face fell. "I guess that was a stupid question."

Aidan linked with me. *We've got to get Logan's and Gabby's attitudes in check. They're dicks half the time. And after what Logan pulled back there ...*He trailed off.

He didn't have to say more. I was just as upset as he was about Logan killing the alpha. At least, that had removed Honor and Ada's pack connection. They formed a small pack within themselves with Honor as the alpha, so they wouldn't go too insane. They didn't have any mates to ground them like the others.

They've gotten worse since they mated. They must have begun feeding off each other, so I took it upon myself to make Honor feel better. "It's not a stupid question at all. Gabby doesn't like it when others question her intelligence."

Gabby growled low, but that was it.

"Have you ever wanted something so much it felt like you had to have it? Like you may not be able to survive without it." It was a hard feeling to describe.

"Yeah, leaving that asshole pack." Honor pointed at Ada. "We've been desperate to leave for years, but I feel terrible for leaving the others behind."

"Well, it kind of feels like that. You feel a desperate

need to be near the chosen girl ... if that makes sense." I didn't know how else to explain it. "And don't worry; when we find this last girl, we'll save your pack. After all, we will be their alphas."

"Thank God we can save them. Even though the alpha died, all the other men are just as bad if not worse." Honor ran a hand down her face. "It was so hard growing up there."

"And they didn't allow us to bring others in, so recently, family members began mating together." Ada shivered. "Like at the cousin level, but it won't be much longer before it becomes closer than that."

The thought revolted me. "Well, that won't be a problem soon."

We were north of Austin, and I began to scan the roads. It was stupid, but I almost expected the girl to just appear on the side of the road, waiting for us to pick her up. Luck would never be on my side like that.

We were nearly twenty miles outside of Austin when something tugged deep inside. "Wait ..." I sat straight in my seat.

"You got something?" Aidan glanced at me as his hands tightened on the steering wheel.

"Yeah. Do you two feel it too?" I glanced over my shoulder.

Gabby nodded, and Honor took deep, rapid breaths.

"I think I do ..." Honor half laughed. "It's so odd."

"Turn off here." A sign to Georgetown popped up on the side of the road. "That's where we need to go." I felt it deep in my bones.

"Okay." Aidan took the exit heading toward the heart of the town.

My phone rang, and I didn't have to look at it to know who it was. "I'm assuming Ivory felt the same thing?"

"Yup. Just making sure we were all on the same page. I'll let you go so you guys can concentrate."

"Sounds good." I ended the call and put the phone in the cupholder. I opened myself up as much as possible, waiting for the tug to strengthen.

We drove through a cute little town surrounded by trees. That made sense since we were looking for a wolf.

Small, quaint brick buildings lined the downtown roads. They were well kept, and people were bustling through it. The town was very picturesque.

Not even five blocks from downtown, signs pointed to a lagoon and hiking trail. "We need to stop here." It made sense to begin here.

Aidan followed my instructions, and we pulled into a full parking lot. We drove to the farthest corner, passing by a huge swimming hole crowded with people. Limestone bluffs made the view spectacular, and several people were swimming under a mini waterfall. The water stretched for miles, and deep woods surrounded it.

Samuel pulled beside us, and we piled out of the vehicles, heading to the tree line.

"She's definitely this way," Ivory stated as we hurried into the woods.

"She won't be on the main trail, so we need to be careful." Luckily, we'd entered into a heavily wooded area not designated for hiking.

Gabby turned to Logan. "Do you three want to shift again?"

That's not happening this time. Aidan growled through our bond. Right before he could open his mouth to respond, I jumped in.

"How about we all go as human?" If Aidan had suggested it, Logan would've put up a fight, and I needed to keep their emotions leveled. "Worst case, the three of you shift again and we carry your clothes back to the car, or, hell, you put on what you have and we go buy another outfit later."

"Fine." Logan's jaw clenched, but he didn't say another word.

I think he's afraid you'll follow through on your promise of leaving him behind. Aidan took my hand. *Did I mention you were hot as hell, putting them in their place the other night?*

Yes, you have. Multiple times. I squeezed his hand and kissed him before moving forward. *Together, we're a team. Don't forget it.*

Our group walked in silence, which was preferable. There was no telling what we might stumble upon.

The tugging grew stronger and stronger with each step we took. Soon, the faint scent of wolves filled the air.

We were getting close.

Aidan linked with me again. *So, I'm thinking this will be The Hallowed Guild. My dad occasionally talked about an Austin branch, so the location north of the city makes sense, especially with this kind of area.*

He was right. The pack could run free in these woods. *The tugging is leading me to the wolf scents.*

I turned to the witches and placed my finger to my lips. We hadn't spoken, but they needed to know we were getting close and that wolves were nearby.

The tree line thinned, which didn't surprise me. They probably lived in a small neighborhood like most other packs. Honor's pack was a little unusual, but a handful of shifters still preferred surviving in the woods.

As we drew closer, the wolves' scents blended together. This had to be a decent-sized pack, which didn't bode well for us.

The sounds of people talking reached our ears. It didn't take long before the voices were clear.

"We found her in town," an older man said. "She was at a tattoo parlor, wanting him to cover up her mark. Little did she know, the pack runs the shop."

"It's a damn good thing," a younger man replied. "Dad was right, that the shop would come in handy one day. Where is she now?"

"She's out near the woods, chained to a tree." The older man sounded so proud. "I figured our new alpha would want to kill her."

Honor's eyes widened and looked at me.

She was expecting me to do something, but there wasn't much I could do. We had to get closer to check it all out.

Houses came into view, and Aidan stopped and lifted a hand. We were on a hill that overlooked a group of thirty shifters down by a huge house. A girl was chained to a tree by her hands and ankles. It reminded me of a dog chained up outside. With her back to the tree trunk, she could move her arms and legs, but the farther she walked away, the more restrained the chains got.

Long blonde hair a shade lighter than mine fell down her arms as she yanked against the chains, trying to escape.

An older man with little hair stepped forward and grinned, revealing five missing teeth. "There's no use, abomination. You're not getting free." He was taller than her but had a huge belly.

It took a lot for a shifter to get fat, even in old age. He must have been dedicated to the cause.

"Look, I'm not here to hurt anyone." She turned around and yanked on the chains again. "I'm not a risk to you."

"Then why were you trying to hide the mark behind your ear?" Another older man stepped from the crowd. He wore a black suit, and his hair was gelled back. His appearance was a stark contrast to the gross man beside him.

"Because it just appeared a few weeks ago, and I don't know why." The girl's blue eyes widened in fear. "It freaked me the hell out, so I wanted to hide it."

"And it should scare you." The well-dressed guy ran his fingers through her hair. "But don't worry, we'll help you. It's just a damn shame that you're a looker."

"Wait ... what do you mean, 'help me'?" Her bottom lip quivered.

What the hell can we do? I couldn't let them hurt her, but dammit, we were outnumbered.

I ... I don't know. Aidan glanced around, trying to figure something out.

A door shut, and a tall guy appeared. He had light brown hair gelled straight up and stubble above his lip and all along his chin. His t-shirt wasn't tight, but it molded to his muscles, and his jeans defined his muscular legs. He towered over every single man as he focused on the girl. "This is her?"

I could have sworn he sounded surprised, but I was sure I was mistaken. His expression hadn't changed.

"Yes. She came into my shop, and I saw the mark." The guy in the suit nodded as he pulled out a blade.

We have to do something. I took a step, but Aidan grabbed my arm.

If we do something, we'll all die. Aidan's voice cracked, and his forehead creased with worry.

Honor stepped forward, but Samuel pulled her against his chest.

Everyone knew we didn't have the upper hand—or hell, any hand at all.

"You get the honors." The man in the suit handed the blade to the guy in front of him.

The guy paused, and the man in the suit arched an eyebrow and asked, "Is there a problem?"

"What? No." The guy took the blade and walked straight up to the girl.

"I don't mean any harm." The girl backed away and butted up against the tree trunk.

No, we have to try. If we lost a single girl, we couldn't fulfill the prophecy, and we'd be screwed. I took a step forward, causing a branch to snap, and Amethyst jumped forward, blocking me from view.

What was she doing? I couldn't let her die over my carelessness.

A wolf looked at us before I could get back in front of her. I was ready for a war cry, but none came. How was that possible?

Amethyst took a step in front of us and faced our group, placing a finger to her lips.

That's when it clicked. She used magic to hide us.

"Kill her before her pack gets here." The guy in the suit looked back at the tall guy.

The tall guy nodded and walked to the girl. Tears ran down her face.

"You won't be a threat to our kind any longer." He swung the dagger across her neck, cutting it. Blood poured from the cut and ran down her shirt. The girl clutched her throat, terror clear in her eyes.

That was it. We'd lost. We had failed to save her.

CHAPTER TWENTY-TWO

"So do we watch the life drain out of her?" The potbelly wolf chuckled with hope.

"She's still a shifter," the tall man responded as his eyes flashed with something I couldn't discern. He threw the bloody dagger to the ground. "She deserves a little respect."

"Like hell, she does," the older guy growled. "If your father was still alive ..."

"But he's not." The tall young man spun around and stared down potbelly man. "So you can stop right there before we have a problem."

"Hugo, you better not push," the suit guy muttered to the potbelly man beside him.

Hugo. That was his name. His mom really hadn't given him a chance, or maybe he was trying to live up to the name. It had to be one or the other.

"Fine. Where are you going to take her?" Hugo's eyes went back to the girl. A smirk filled his face as he watched blood pour between her fingers.

"I'll take her to the woods and bury her." The tall man walked over to the girl. "Where's the key?"

"Here." The suit tossed him the keys.

How long do you think she has? I felt hopeless. We'd come all this way for nothing. How the hell could we finish this curse if we couldn't reveal the next set of pages?

I don't know. Aidan took my hand and squeezed. *But we'll do every damn thing we can for her.*

I glanced at the three girls beside me. Pure agony filled their faces. I wasn't the only one who'd lost hope.

Tears poured down the girl's face as she clutched her neck to stop the bleeding. Her hands, shirt, and even her jeans were drenched in blood. Hell, there was so much blood that the metallic scent saturated the air where we were.

The huge guy moved closer to her. She flinched and fell to her ass. He ignored her and unchained her wrists and ankles.

She scooted away from him, her hands slipping from her throat.

Several deep chuckles came from the onlookers.

It made me sick. These were the depraved type of people who enjoyed watching their own kind die right in front of their eyes? Any chance of us fixing things was dwindling with every second.

"Stop fighting me." The tall man grabbed the girl by the waist. "You'll only make things worse."

"How many men do you want to go with you?" the suit asked as the man threw the girl over her shoulder.

Now blood flowed down her face and into her hair.

"No, just me." The tall guy took off into the woods, heading to our left. "I need to question her before she's too far gone. I'll alert you if I need backup." The guy didn't stop walking or bother turning back to ensure they'd listened. He expected them to.

This was our only chance. Maybe Amethyst could heal her enough to save her life. Granted, if it was a fatal wound, no witch could undo the damage.

I leaned over and motioned for the group to follow him. Ivory was at the far end and understood immediately. She took off in the alpha's direction, making sure to keep a slow enough pace so the witches could be careful.

We intercepted the alpha's scent and followed closely behind. As long as the breeze didn't shift, he wouldn't smell us until it was too late.

Our group could easily overtake one wolf shifter if we hit him hard before he alerted the pack. If he contacted his pack, we'd have to get the hell out of there before his backup arrived.

The woods grew denser again as we hurried for several long minutes. If it hadn't been for his strong scent, we would've lost him. *How far away will he take her from the pack?* I'd expected maybe a mile or two, tops.

Not sure, but this is strange. Aidan was right behind me, keeping an eye out for any threats that might come from behind. *He has to be up to something.*

That was my thinking as well.

Ivory lifted her hand and pointed in front of her.

I was sure we must be close. Our group spread out amongst the trees but kept in sight of one another.

I looked at the girl. Blood covered her face. With shaky hands, she used her sleeve to try to wipe it out from her eyes.

"What ..." She paused and winced, clutching her neck once more. She tried again. "What do you want?" Pain flicked through her eyes, and her shoulders sagged, but her fierce will to survive was strong. "I'm not telling you shit. It's not like it'll do me any good."

"Stop with the dramatics." The tall guy rolled his eyes. "We've got to figure a way out of this mess."

"What are you talking about?" The girl's chest heaved as if she were holding a sob in.

"If I wanted to kill you, you'd be dead right now, not talking." The alpha guy blew out a breath and frowned.

"Wait ... I'm bleeding out here." The girl removed her hands from her throat and looked at the red that covered them.

"It's a superficial cut. I didn't hit an artery. You're fine." The guy's voice was gruff.

Holy shit. This couldn't be true ... could it? There was only one way to find out. Hope sprung throughout my chest once more. I stepped out from behind the tree, alerting them to my presence.

Dammit, Emma. Aidan growled as he moved beside me.

The alpha turned and narrowed his eyes at me. "Who the hell are you two?"

"We're not here to cause trouble, we're just here for her." I pointed to the girl.

His jade eyes flashed at the girl. "Are they part of your pack?"

"What? No." She shook her head and stared at me. "I've never seen them before in my life."

The breeze changed directions, and the alpha stiffened as he sniffed the air. "How many of you are there?"

I guessed our jig was up.

The other ten stepped from the shadows.

"I can call my pack." The tall guy scowled at me.

"Bullshit." He was trying to alpha me, and I couldn't let it happen. I stepped closer to him, wanting him to know he didn't intimidate me. The closer I got, the more I realized Aidan had an inch on him.

The guy's eyes narrowed, and something like respect flashed in them. "What do you want?"

"Her." Aidan stepped beside me, wanting to make it clear we were a package deal. "We don't give a shit about you or your pack."

"Oh, that's so comforting." The guy crossed his arms. "You're not getting her."

"You fucking cut me." The girl's eyes widened, and she stumbled in my direction. "I'd rather take my chances with them."

"Look, my pack can't find out I didn't kill you." The guy paced.

Gabby arched an eyebrow. "Then why did you save her?"

"I don't know." The guy grabbed a fistful of his hair. "I had every damn intention of killing her, but when I went for it ... I couldn't."

Do you think she's his mate? It was a pattern.

Maybe. Aidan nibbled on his bottom lip. *We can use this to our advantage.*

"You still cut me, psycho," the girl growled and winced.

"To protect you," The alpha huffed. "If I hadn't, they would've taken matters into their own hands and killed you on the spot."

"He's right about that." Remus nodded. "They're The Hallowed Guild."

"How do you know that?" The alpha stiffened, and his jaw clenched.

"Because we were part of the society too." Remus pointed at Ivory and then himself.

"And so was I." Aidan nodded. *Don't mention who my father is. I don't trust him.*

"May I heal her?" Amethyst took a hesitant step

forward, ready for disgust to cross the alpha's face.

He didn't disappoint as he lifted his head with a scowl. "Fine, but I'm watching you."

The girl smiled as Amethyst slowly walked over to her.

"At least she doesn't seem to hate us," Coral grumbled, not happy with the alpha's reaction.

"If you're part of the society, how are you here with them?" The alpha turned his nose up at the red-headed witch.

"Because we found our mates who ..." Aidan trailed off. *Maybe we shouldn't ...*

No, I agreed with his initial decision. "Their mates are marked."

"Wait ... all of you are?" He eyed every single girl in the group. "I thought there were only five or something like that. But you're saying there's nine?"

"Oh, no." I hadn't considered that he'd think every female here was marked. "Just the female hybrids. Beth and Ada are full shifters, and those two ladies are pure witches."

"Will it hurt?" the girl asked as Amethyst placed her hands on her neck wound.

"No, dear. I promise." Amethyst smiled. "What's your name?"

"Sunny." Her voice sounded so raw.

"That's a beautiful name." Amethyst's voice was calming as magic filled the air.

"What's your name?" Logan lifted a brow at the alpha guy.

"It's Eric." His eyes stayed glued on Sunny and Amethyst. "Do I get the pleasure of knowing all your names?"

Beth took the liberty of introducing us.

"There, you're all done." Amethyst lifted her hand from

her neck. A scab remained where the cut had been.

Sunny tentatively touched her neck. "Thank you."

"See, witches aren't all bad." Samuel puffed out his chest to appear larger.

"Look, you don't have many options here." Honor held out her hand. "What are you going to do with her?"

"I ... I don't know." Eric rubbed a hand down his face. "I just don't understand why I couldn't kill her."

"Wow, that's so romantic," Ada snorted. "Guys are assholes."

In all fairness, Aidan had been an asshole for over four years. I couldn't argue too much.

"Look, the longer we wait out here, the likelier a wolf will come looking for you," Ivory said softly. "It's best if she comes with us."

"I don't want her to go," Eric grumbled as he kicked the ground.

"If you don't want her to die, she needs to come with us," I explained, hoping to show him logic, something he couldn't dispute. "We'll take care of her."

"That sounds nice." Sunny sighed. "After my pack turned me away ..."

"What do you mean your pack turned you away?" Coral asked, an edge to her steady voice.

"I was raised there, but when they saw the mark, the alpha denounced me." Sunny grimaced. "They didn't want to deal with the fallout, but they wouldn't tell me what it meant either. My dad died last year, so I have no one to stand up for me. That's why I was trying to cover the mark. It has to mean something bad."

"She's not safe here." Aidan looked at the alpha. "We can protect her."

"Fine." Eric inhaled sharply as he walked over and

paused. "This is fucking crazy. I already miss her, and I've known her less than thirty minutes." He pulled Sunny into his arms and lowered his nose, smelling her bloodstained hair.

Her eyes widened as her hand inched up to hug him back, but she forcibly dropped it by her side. Confusion was etched on her face.

"But I need to be able to contact her," Eric said as his eyes met mine. "I need to be able to check in on her."

"Fine." I'd do anything to get her to leave, and if I pushed too hard, he'd make things difficult.

She pulled back slightly from his arms and retrieved her phone from her pocket. "Here ..."

"No, we're leaving your phone behind." Aidan took the phone out of her hand and threw it on the ground. "If someone gets hold of your old pack, they could track you. We can get you a new phone later." Aidan crushed the phone with the heel of his foot.

Approval shone in Eric's eyes. "Maybe she will be safer in your hands."

"For the time being, use mine." I handed my phone to him. "Call yourself, then we'll have each other's numbers."

"Fine." He dialed a number, let it ring once, and hung up. As he handed it back to me, he tensed. "Shit, they're coming."

Not wasting time, I reared back and punched him straight in the nose. It cracked loudly.

"What the hell, Emma?" Samuel hollered. He blinked like he couldn't believe his eyes.

Aidan chuckled. "Well, she beat me to the punch."

Blood poured out Eric's nose, and he nodded at me with respect. "Again, and then you all need to run as fast as possible."

"Let me." Sunny rammed her knee right into his crotch, and he fell to the ground in pain.

"Holy shit," he groaned, tears springing to his eyes.

She kissed his cheek. "That's what you get for cutting me."

"Is this normal?" Coral glanced from Sunny to Eric.

"It is when we need the wolves to think he put up a fight." I waved them on. "Let's go."

Our group moved out, with Sunny, Aidan, and me hanging back. I took her hand. "You can call him tonight, but right now, we have to go."

"Fine." She glanced at him one last time. "Don't die, okay?"

"I'll try not to," he said through clenched teeth.

Sunny took off, and I followed, with Aidan taking up the rear. Our group ran as fast as we could without worrying about noise. The wolves would check on Eric first, and he should buy us some time.

Halfway to the car, I heard running footsteps in the distance behind us. *Dammit, they're catching up to us.* I'd hoped we would be closer to the vehicles.

They know the woods, so they have the advantage. Aidan didn't even bother turning around. They were at least ten miles behind but gaining ground. "Hurry up."

Remus was leading the charge, and he took off even faster.

"Everyone, run as fast as you can." We'd have to slow down for the witches, but hopefully, the three of them could run a little faster.

With each step we took, the wolves caught up by two. I hated feeling like prey, but dammit, that's exactly what we were.

The trees flew by as we pushed ourselves to the max

without trampling over the witches.

The wolves' heavy breathing became audible. They were literally breathing down our necks. We wouldn't make it to the car before they caught up to us.

"Everyone, keep going!" I shouted. "Get in the cars." The guys liked fighting, but Remus and Logan were too far in front.

Yes, those idiots would hear us, but it sounded like there were only two chasing us. More might be on their way, but we should be able to keep these morons at bay.

The clearing came into view, and we exited the woods, away from the humans.

Aidan spun around and ran right at a wolf as it lunged through the air. He lowered his body to the ground and raised up right as the wolf was about to attack him. He pushed his arms forward, and the wolf flew backward, hitting the ground hard on his back.

The second wolf charged in as Aidan fought off the first wolf.

Oh, hell no. I pushed my legs as hard as I could and steamrolled the wolf right in the side. It hadn't expected the force and stumbled, unable to turn and use its claws against me. I slammed it hard against a tree as the first wolf bounced back onto its legs.

If you get hurt, let me know immediately.

Aidan's words surprised me. A short time ago, he'd begged for me to leave and not fight. The fact that he was accepting me as an equal meant way too damn much. There was no way in hell I would jeopardize that.

As the second wolf shook its auburn head, I grabbed a fallen tree branch, ran over, and smacked it hard in the head. It crashed to the ground.

I spun around to find the other wolf's teeth locked

around Aidan's upper arm. *What the hell?*

Blood spewed everywhere and already coated the ground. I rushed over to the wolf right as it tugged hard on his arm, trying to tear it off.

I raised the branch above my head, focused on the one spot that would do the worst damage, aiming to smack the wolf in the jaw.

He saw me coming, let go of Aidan's arm, and turned toward me with a snarl. He bared blood-covered teeth at me; the metallic scent of my mate's blood churned my stomach worse than normal.

"You son of a bitch!" I yelled as if the words would inflict pain, but the wolf only chuckled ... or at least that's what it sounded like.

We were too close to not make it out of this alive. I ran harder, heading right at the wolf, playing a game of chicken.

"Emma, what are you doing?" Pain laced Aidan's words, telling me he was in more pain than he was letting on.

I ignored him; this was between me and the wolf. As I got closer, the wolf stood on his hind legs, ready to wrench the thick branch from my grasp. The moment I met up with him, I let Sunny inspire me and kicked the wolf square in the nuts.

As he crashed to the ground as Eric had, I raised the branch and swung down hard.

No one hurt my mate. No one.

I raced over to Aidan. "Let's go."

"At least he can't reproduce anymore." He shook his head in awe despite the lines of pain etched on his face.

"Let's get going before more show up. We need to get you healed and head back home." Right now, Amethyst's coven felt like home, and we needed to get there desperately.

CHAPTER TWENTY-THREE

With how drenched in blood Sunny was and Aidan's injury, we decided to drive straight back to Columbus, Georgia. Luckily, it was only a fourteen-hour drive.

Twenty or so miles from the attack, we pulled over, and Amethyst laid her hands on Aidan, healing some of the wound. She stopped the bleeding, but the wound was still tender, and he struggled to move his arm. Beth took over driving, and I stayed in the back with him and Honor. Ada took my spot in the passenger front seat.

On the way home, we didn't stop unless for necessities. To keep away from humans, we'd used nature for the bathroom, and we only went through drive-thrus for food; we'd hid Sunny and Aidan in the back to avoid alarming the fast-food workers. We didn't need them freaking out and calling the police. The less commotion we caused, the less likely we'd be found by The Hallowed Guild.

We rolled into town late at night. A sense of peace came over me as I spotted the coven homes. I hadn't felt that in a long time, but after the shitshow we'd gone through, I felt safe here with them. I hadn't noticed how much I trusted them until this second.

"What is this place?" Honor looked out the window at the homes in a neighborhood in the middle of nowhere.

"It's Amethyst's coven." I squirmed in the middle seat. Being in the back bench seats for the past thirteen hours had been truly uncomfortable. I tried not to put too much weight on Aidan given how badly he was hurting, and I tried not to complain—we had a full vehicle. "I guess, technically, it's my coven too. My mom was a member before her death."

"Oh, and you found each other?" Ada turned around in the front to glance at me. "How so?"

"Actually, we all met at Crawford University." I pointed to Beth. "Including that crazy one up there."

Beth pulled into Beatrice's driveway and looked in the rearview mirror. "And you love me the most out of all of 'em."

"Shh." I winked at her and nodded my head at Aidan. "He might hear you."

"You two realize I'm neither deaf nor blind—just injured." A smile spread across Aidan's lips.

"You could be delusional." I stuck my tongue out at him.

"As lovey-dovey as this is, I'm leaving," Logan grumbled and opened the door.

"Don't leave me behind." Gabby climbed out after him.

"Are they always that way?" Ada asked.

"Probably better since Emma put them in their place after Logan killed your alpha." Beth shrugged.

The rest of our group exited the vehicle, and we joined the others. Beatrice, Finn, Rowan, and Sage walked out the front door.

"Oh my Goddess." Beatrice hurried over to us as she took in Sunny and Aidan. "Are you two okay?"

"Mom, I told you there was an incident and it looked really bad," Amethyst replied with a yawn.

"Are any of them still bleeding?" Finn grinned as he looked at the two shifters.

"You can't be serious." Aidan shook his head. "I see nothing has changed."

"Bleeding wolves bring a smile to my face." Finn shrugged, and his smile grew bigger.

"And you wondered why you couldn't join us." Coral's nose wrinkled.

"Hey ..." Finn's jaw clenched, and he took a step toward Coral.

"Calm your ass down, *cousin*." I grabbed his arm and pulled him hard against me. "I'm tired of your unhelpful attitude. Shut it before I make you." Between him, Logan, and Gabby, I was so close to snapping. Their attitudes had to go and now.

His breathing increased as he stared into my eyes. My wolf surged forward in response, and he glanced down, submitting.

Amethyst cleared her throat, trying to divert the attention off me. "Aidan is still injured. I used too much of my magic on Sunny less than an hour before." Amethyst frowned. "Can you finish the job?"

"Of course, dear." Beatrice placed a hand on Aidan's uninjured arm. "It would be my honor." She waved to the group with her other hand. "Let's get everyone situated. We can reconvene in the morning."

I wanted to argue, but Aidan being healed was far more important.

"You two can stay with us ..." Rowan started, pointing at Honor.

"No, I'm sorry. I came here because of Emma." Honor gestured to me. "I want to stay close to her."

"Same." Gabby crossed her arms. "I don't want to be separated."

"You heard—" Finn started, but Beatrice lifted her hand, cutting him off.

"That's fine." She turned toward Amethyst. "Dear, can you, Samuel, and Coral go get the blow-up mattresses and set them up in the living room?"

"But you don't know anything about them." Finn's shoulders stiffened. "It's not safe ..."

"Did you forget who the leader is here?" Beatrice's voice was cold and so unlike her. She lifted her chin and narrowed her eyes at my cousin.

He sucked in a breath. "No, I did not."

"Good. Now, help the others get the mattresses ready," Beatrice said with authority.

"Come on, man." Samuel yanked on Finn's arm.

Sage walked over and kissed Samuel's cheek. "They're in the closet downstairs."

"Okay, Mom." Samuel took the lead, and the other three followed after him.

"Let's go on inside." Beatrice walked to the front door and opened it. "There are three showers, so please make yourselves at home."

"I call dibs." Sunny pulled at her matted, blood-drenched blonde hair. "I need this out now."

Everyone carried their stuff inside the house and rotated out of the showers as Beatrice, Amethyst, Aidan, and I sat at the kitchen table.

"It's best if you remove your shirt so I can touch the wound directly." Beatrice's gaze settled on me.

"I'll help." I stood and helped Aidan slowly pull his shirt away. The material had gotten stuck to the wound because of the dried blood.

I peeled it away as gently as possible, but he winced at each movement.

"I'm so sorry." I felt horrible.

"It's not your fault." He forced a smile. "If it weren't for you, I'd be dead."

"I highly doubt that." He was so strong. I suspected there wasn't anyone he couldn't take.

"No, with this injury, I would've been." He nibbled his bottom lip, and his golden eyes were so dark they were almost brown. "Just yank it off."

"But it might make your injury worse." I hated causing him pain.

"Which Beatrice will heal soon. Let's just yank it off like a Band-Aid." *I promise it'll be okay.*

"Here, let me help." Beatrice placed her hands on the part of the injury she could touch. "This should do the trick." She closed her eyes, and once again, the buzzing of magic in the air brushed against my skin, energizing my blood.

Her hand glowed white as she pushed magic into Aidan's shoulder, and I watched in wonder as the skin mended around her hand.

In a few minutes, he was completely healed, and we were getting ready for bed.

I understood why we were waiting until later this morning to activate the diary, but sleep evaded me. The past couple of weeks had been focused on finding the girls and getting back here to see what the next steps were, so to wait even longer was almost unbearable.

Aidan was sleeping more soundly than usual, probably because of his injury. Even though Beatrice had healed most of it, it had taken a lot out of him.

Not wanting my tossing and turning to wake him, I crawled out of bed, quietly padded out of the room, and tiptoed past the den where the four girls, Logan, Remus, and Ada slept.

In the kitchen, I opened the back door wide enough to slip through. I shut it and waited to see if anyone followed me.

After a few seconds, I let go of the breath I was holding. For the first time in weeks, I was alone. It felt foreign but nice.

I headed to the woods and walked along the tree line. The moon shone, and I closed my eyes, enjoying the breeze.

Finn's voice drifted through the air. "Prescott, they're here."

All sense of peace vanished, and my body tensed. I picked up my pace, heading toward the edge of the neighborhood. I stopped short when Finn came into view.

He ran a hand through his auburn hair, glancing around erratically. "No, I won't tell you where we are. I have my coven and cousin to protect."

Why was he bringing me up?

"Look, I'll give you information when I can, but they found the other four girls." Finn spun around, facing in my direction, except his human eyes couldn't find me.

"No, they didn't let me go and didn't tell us where each

one was located; that's why I couldn't give you the information." He huffed. "Look, as long as you promise I get to kill the Murphy alpha and my cousin remains unharmed, I'm down to help you, but we can't be reckless. My coven can't know what I'm doing. The priestess would banish me."

I had so many questions. The Hallowed Guild hated witches, so none of this made sense.

"I've got to go, but I'll call you when I have something you can use." Finn ended the call and glanced around again.

Humans could always tell when they were being watched even if they didn't understand what they were feeling. He ran off toward Sage's house, leaving me alone in the woods.

My own family was betraying me. This could only mean one thing: this was a war, and I didn't know all of the players. The more I learned, the more unclear everything became. But they didn't know the wrath of Emma, and when they felt it, they would all cower in fear.

The End

ABOUT THE AUTHOR

Jen L. Grey is a *USA Today* Bestselling Author who writes Paranormal Romance, Urban Fantasy, and Fantasy genres.

Jen lives in Tennessee with her husband, two daughters, and two miniature Australian Shepherd. Before she began writing, she was an avid reader and enjoyed being involved in the indie community. Her love for books eventually led her to writing. For more information, please visit her website and sign up for her newsletter.

Check out my future projects and book signing events at my website.
www.jenlgrey.com

ALSO BY JEN L. GREY

The Marked Wolf Trilogy
Moon Kissed
Chosen Wolf
Broken Curse

Wolf Moon Academy Trilogy
Shadow Mate
Blood Legacy
Rising Fate

The Royal Heir Trilogy
Wolves' Queen
Wolf Unleashed
Wolf's Claim

Bloodshed Academy Trilogy
Year One
Year Two
Year Three

The Half-Breed Prison Duology (Same World As Bloodshed Academy)
Hunted
Cursed

The Artifact Reaper Series

Reaper: The Beginning

Reaper of Earth

Reaper of Wings

Reaper of Flames

Reaper of Water

Stones of Amaria (Shared World)

Kingdom of Storms

Kingdom of Shadows

Kingdom of Ruins

Kingdom of Fire

The Pearson Prophecy

Dawning Ascent

Enlightened Ascent

Reigning Ascent

Stand Alones

Death's Angel

Rising Alpha

Printed in Great Britain
by Amazon